CHRISTMAS JOY

A Sweet Christmas Volume 4

SAMANTHA JACOBEY

Lavish Publishing LLC

First Edition

A Sweet Christmas Series Book 4

2018 Lavish Publishing, LLC

Published in the United States by Lavish Publishing, LLC, Midland, TX

Cover Design by: Victor R. Sosa

Cover Images: CanStock

Paperback Edition

ISBN: 978-1-944985-67-7

www.LavishPublishing.com

Contents

Prologue

"WE'LL NEED to replace these stairs," Gary pointed out. Using his pencil, he indicated the narrow wooden slats that had connected the kitchen to the basement for decades.

"Yeah," Candy sighed, thinking of the first time she had come down them. Her mother and son had been in the hospital after a fire nearly killed them. The memory sending a shudder through her, she crossed her arms over her chest and gave herself a squeeze. "The list is going to be long."

"It already is," Gerald agreed, adding the words *basement stairs* on line number forty-four of his bright yellow pages. "But we have to meet all their requirements, or we won't be approved."

Flicking a brief smile at him, Candy's heart fluttered. As of this past Christmas, she and Gary had been married just over a year and had lived under the same roof for a second year before that. It had taken him months to convince her to even date him, and now they were looking to adopt a baby together.

"Thank you for doing this," she said in a timid voice.

"No problem, kitten," he replied in a distracted manner, still inspecting his list and only half hearing her comment.

After Christmas had come and gone, things had settled into a routine in the Ford household. Caroline had stayed on as their fulltime nanny and housekeeper, allowing Candy to continue her schoolwork and for Dakota to receive the best of care possible. Lanelle was also doing well, and it seemed like the perfect time to discuss expanding their family, but Candy's doubts about carrying another child had put a crimp in those plans.

As a compromise, the pair had decided that adopting was their best option, taking some of the pressure off the young woman and alleviating her fears of repeating the illness that had irreparably changed her son's life forever. Candy had learned the hard way how seemingly small decisions could have a profound impact on a person's life, and she felt certain their current plans would alter their lives together in ways they had not yet realized.

Shifting her eyes around, she felt driven to make the best of the State's demands and include changes she would enjoy. "Shall we get a new washer and dryer while we're at it?" she asked coyly.

"Do we really need them?" Gary coughed, eyeing their current machines.

"Well, you know," Candy cooed, sidling up to him and running her fingers over the material of his pressed shirt, "if we are going to adopt, we could end up with two or three additions to the family. We do want to give everyone clean clothes even with our expanding numbers."

Gary grinned at her playfulness, well aware their current laundry facilities were probably just fine for the task. However, she had been pretty cooperative since he had agreed her fear of carrying and delivering another baby were justified. Besides, adopting a child would be every bit as rewarding as having his own, and in some ways, even more so. "Number forty-five, washer and dryer," he mumbled as his pencil scrawled.

"Thanks," Candice clipped, her hair floating as she spun and inspected the walls. "You know, it is kind of odd that they want every part of the house 'child proofed' and ready. We'll be getting a baby, after all. What would he or she be doing in the basement?"

"We don't know that for certain," he replied quietly. "Older children need homes, too. I mean, we can request a baby, but they are much harder to come by, as there are far more foster parents who want a baby than there are infants to fill the homes. Let's get through the approval process before we start dreaming of what our new member is going to look or be like."

"That's good advice," Carol agreed from half-way down the stairs. "You missed a call from the agency, but I took a message," she offered with a smile.

"What's the message?" Gary asked, dropping his legal pad to his side and bouncing it anxiously as he gazed up at her.

"They want an estimate for setting your inspection date. Ms. Tucker said it can be changed later, but it will help her organize her calendar if you have a guess."

Glancing at his wife, Gary swallowed. "Our list is

pretty extensive," he admitted in a hushed tone. "And I'm sure we have more to add."

"Lots more." Candy nodded, inhaling deeply through flared nostrils at the thought of the months ahead. "I'll be busy with school, too, so it may take even longer than normal." She was doing this for Gary, after all, so the longer they put it off, the better off they would be.

His gut twisting, Gary took a step closer to their housekeeper and directed, "Call her back and tell her to give us a December date. We'll do our best to have it all done by then, and I'm sure she'll be checking our progress along the way."

"No doubt," Candy mumbled, having seen the list of requirements prospective adopters had to meet. She had hoped Gary would use his money and family's influence to fund a private adoption, but he had insisted they go through the public system.

"Yes," he agreed, smiling broadly to ward off her foreboding as he took to the stairs. "Thanks, Carol. I'll call her back myself and get us on the books. Then I'll get this list to our contractor and see when they can begin," he informed the two women as he exited the top with Carol close behind.

Alone in the musty space, Candy sighed. She still wasn't certain how all of this was going to work out, and the idea of having their inspection so close to the holiday did not put her mind at ease. Christmas had never been kind to her, and she had little evidence her luck would be any different this year, despite her efforts to the contrary.

ONE

A Choice for Life

HALLOWEEN MORNING, Gary's head swam with plans for the evening as he drove his Suburban to the station. His extended family would be gathering for their annual dinner, and the house had been bustling with preparations as he left that morning, putting him a little late getting to his post.

Most of the renovations they had deemed necessary last spring were complete, thankfully, but there was still quite a bit to be done before all of their "I"s had been dotted and "T"s had been crossed. This decision had been a choice for life, and therefore he and Candy had taken it very seriously, including ensuring all the requirements had been met with due diligence, despite the inconvenience.

"Still," he said aloud to himself, "we'll soon have a baby in the house." He couldn't know for certain how long it would take, but their appointment for final inspection had been slated for the first week of December, and it was getting closer every day.

Turning into the parking lot adjacent to the firehouse, he drew a deep breath to calm his excitement. He could tell that Candy had been a lot less enthusiastic than he had been through the process, despite her efforts to hide her trepidation. He felt certain most of that was due to the stress of taking care of her schoolwork and still making time for her family as it was. *Having a new member is only going to make that worse,* he surmised, confident she would make it through.

Exiting the vehicle, he felt calmer as he strode around to the front of the station and entered through the wide-open door. Spying Tom enjoying the morning in the opening, he gave the crewman a wave and called in a playful manner, “Is that coffee fresh?”

“Just brewed,” Tom sang, raising his mug to him in a mock toast.

Tom had followed him to the location only a few weeks after Gary had taken over as the chief, and it felt good having his old comrade there with him at the new station. “Perfect.” Gary grinned to himself as he made a straight line for the kitchen area to help himself to a cup. As he added a splash of sugar, his phone twittered a short chirp, signaling an incoming message.

Pulling it from his pocket, he glanced at the screen, giving it a swipe with the tip of a finger as he raised the Styrofoam to his lips. “Oh, crap!” he cursed in excited agitation, almost spilling the hot beverage on himself. “Phil, I need you!” he shouted more loudly as he positioned his soft container between the ends of his digits for quicker movement. His palms sweaty as adrenaline surged within, he reached for the handle to his office.

Meeting him there at the door, Phillip Landry queried, “What’s up, boss?”

“The alarm’s been tripped,” Gary spat, pushing the

door open and kicking the block in place to hold it wide. Pausing, he listened to the silence of the room, the only sound the small buzz from the silent alarm that signaled someone had accessed the haven from the outside. On the far wall, a metal door to their new infant box waited, a blinking red light in the corner alerting them that something had indeed been placed inside.

Frozen in place, both staring at the device, Phillip swallowed. "Do you think this is another false alarm?"

"Only one way to find out," Gary replied crisply. Setting his steaming cup on his desk, he pressed the button that would silence the beacon and released the latch. He stepped back, and the hatch slowly opened. Inside, a lump of blanket was all he could see. If an infant lay hidden within, it made no sound or move to alert them to its presence. "Grab a gurney, just in case," he commanded, rubbing his hands together briskly before he pulled the drawer towards him.

"I'll get a med kit, too," Phil agreed. Leaving with a skip in his step, he seized the handle of one of the plastic cases and opened the storage to wheel out one of the mobile beds. Tossing a sheet across it, he gave it a shove towards his would-be patient, if this wasn't another hoax.

"What's going on?" Tom hollered, observing the excitement from his spot where the morning sun landed on the concrete floor at his feet.

"Possible baby in the box," Phil yelled back, setting the med kit on the bed and wheeling it through the propped office door.

Inside, Gary stood holding the bundle against his chest, the weight of it providing evidence that they had indeed received a delivery. Placing the lump on the empty end of the gurney, he began the process of unwrapping the child for an assessment.

As soon as the air hit, the baby began to squirm and stretch, its back arched as it did so. Its moan was slight considering having its nap interrupted, and it concerned Gary that it did not break out into an actual cry.

"Oh," Philip breathed. "This is real."

"Yes, quite real," Gary countered over the sound of his heart pounding in his ears. Their box had been installed during the summer, but the first delivery had been a prank; a plastic doll wrapped in a towel. Those placing items inside one of the containers are assured anonymity, so little had been said about the incident. He felt certain that this one would get a great deal more attention.

Opening its deep blue eyes, the child blinked at them beneath dark rings of hair glued to its scalp and forehead. Shiny in the overhead light, it appeared either damp or to have been oiled and clung to the delicate skin that framed its face. Sucking loudly at the fist that had been firmly imbedded in its mouth, the babe contentedly allowed them their prodding.

"It's only a few days old," Philip stated calmly while pulling out his stethoscope to begin the exam.

"It doesn't appear to be hungry," Gary observed. Watching as Philip gave the heart, lungs, and belly a listen, he offered his finger to the unoccupied hand. The tiny digits closed around it, and he smiled. "Reflexes are good." *Dear God, I can't believe someone used our box*, he added internally. He paused, considering that's exactly why they had installed it, but the reality and finality of the act stole his breath.

Lifting it by the torso, Philip brushed the baby's

little sock-clad feet against the flat surface and noted that it pushed up against it, as if to stand on its pale, bare legs. "Yup, it seems to be in good health. I'm sure they will run a full battery once he's delivered to the hospital."

The belly exposed as he held it, Gary lifted the simple white shirt and peered at the navel. "Cord's tied with yarn. At home birth?" he proposed.

"Likely," Philip agreed, laying it back on the cart and folding the blanket around it. "I'll call the hospital and let them know we'll be down with it shortly."

"Sure," Gary approved, folding the soft material into a cocoon to keep their charge warm in the fall air. As he did so, his fingers brushed against a wad of paper tucked inside the folds of cloth. The baby whimpered, and he scooped it up to his chest once more to comfort it while he inspected his find.

His left arm curled beneath, he held the note in that palm, rocking gently side to side as he uncurled it. Written in orange ink, he could barely make out the words: *Please care for my Joylana. I can't keep her, and she needs someone else to love her.*

"Joylana," he whispered, glancing at the tiny face staring up at him. "So that's who you are." Her small features framed by a yellow blanket, she stared up at him before her eyes slowly closed in a relaxed and trusting fashion.

"We're all set. They're going to send a social worker over to pick him up, though," Philip announced, interrupting with a grin. "I can't believe how easy it was for someone to leave their kid in there."

"I'm sure it wasn't easy at all," Gary countered.

"And it's a her," he added, wafting the note at him. "Joylana."

"Wow, she has a name."

"For now. I bet they change it once she gets in the system," he stated gravely, his thoughts distracted to the preparations he and Candy had been making as he caressed the tiny scalp.

Soon, their home and paperwork would be complete, and they would be on the list of foster parents; people who offered their homes to children such as this. For now, she would end up with someone else who would provide her with everything she needs. Whoever that was would probably adopt her, and she would be theirs for the rest of her life.

"Why so glum?" Tom asked from the door, having kept his distance while he watched the situation unfold.

"Nothing," Gary sighed, using a finger to trace the line of a pudgy jaw. "She's one of the lucky ones, being left here. She'll get a thorough exam at the hospital and medical care if she needs it. She'll be in a new home in a few days."

"I think this baby might be mixed race," Philip observed, returning to his prodding and lightly fingering an ear.

"Maybe," Gary agreed, certain it wouldn't matter. Whoever got her would be happy to have her, and he grinned at the irony of her name. *Joylana is perfect, as she is very likely to bring joy into someone's life very soon.*

TWO

A Family Gathering

WINEGLASS IN HAND, Gary wandered through the crowd of people occupying his living room. The family ritual was in full swing, and a good thirty people filled their newly redecorated living space, including a few who had not been there in recent years. Walking up to one such couple, he offered his hand. "Matthew. Annette. Good that the two of you could make it this year. Are you all settled?"

"As settled as we're going to be," Annette replied stiffly. She was a Ford cousin, and her husband had been chosen to take the VP job Gary had stepped down from in January. Matthew had moved back to town without her, and she had held off making her return. She loved New York City and hated to give it up but was forced to when it became apparent that things were permanent and she would have to come home. "I never thought I would live here again if I were honest," she grunted, cutting her eyes around and scowling at their shared kin.

Gary suppressed a grin at her unspoken assessment. Where the Fords had always had money and privilege, which gave them a certain air, Annette had married well and had taken the next step. Even the Fords no longer seemed good enough for her. "We're glad you're back," he stated simply, observing their only daughter seated on their new couch, cellphone in hand. "Bella seems to be doing well. She's twelve now, isn't she?"

"Yes," Matthew agreed stiffly.

"Not going trick-or-treating with the others?" Eve asked as she and Roger joined them.

"Bah, no," Matt denied. "Begging for candy from strangers isn't really something we have condoned," he added with a disgruntled air.

"It's not about the begging or the candy," Roger replied evenly in his gravelly voice. "It's about sharing the meal with family and getting to know her cousins. They don't see each other often, and they haven't seen Bella in years."

"Well, she won't be joining them," Annette replied in a huff. Seizing her husband's arm, she followed as he led her away from them.

"Wow, they haven't changed at all," Gary observed quietly with a short laugh.

"Not in the slightest," Eve agreed, shaking her head. "I have my sensibilities, but that girl has taken them too far I should think."

"Yes, you should," Gary agreed, offering his mother a toast.

Sipping from the glass, he appeared preoccupied, and Eve studied him coolly. "Has something happened?" she demanded when he spilled no details.

"Nope." Gary shook his head for emphasis, not interested in sharing Joylana's arrival at the station with his mother.

"Very well," she growled. "I'll join your lovely wife and housekeeper in the kitchen. Perhaps their conversation will be more to my liking." Her lips pursed as she walked away, she had disappeared before either of the two men felt free to speak.

"Is something wrong?" Roger prodded.

"Not really, dad. We had a big day at work. That's all," Gary supplied, gulping his glass of wine anxiously. They had not discussed much of their plans with his parents, but with the renovations taking place, they had eventually come clean about the details. Deciding it might be good to talk about it, he confessed, "Someone left a baby in the new box at the station today."

"A real one?" his father gasped.

"Yes. A beautiful little girl. Couldn't be more than a few days old."

"What did Candy say?"

"I didn't tell her," Gary sighed. "She's anxious enough as it is. Besides, another couple will have her in their home long before all our approvals are finalized. Sad to say but there will be another soon enough and we'll have one for ourselves."

"Still, that's a lot to take in," Roger commiserated. "I can see why it bothered you."

"It didn't bother me," Gary chuckled. "I think that's part of the problem. I'm glad her mother left her in our box. Beats the hell out of a trashcan… or worse." His pause long before he added the last thought, Roger stiffened beside him. "That's the thing, dad. These young girls. They end up pregnant and don't know what to do, so they ignore it. If they are able to hide it, no one may even notice that they're expecting, which is sad in itself that no one pays, even that much attention to them.

They pretend it away and when the baby comes they panic."

"That's what the safe haven laws are for," Roger offered, aware of their social issue and his son's small effort to help with their intentions to take in at least one of them soon enough. "Have you decided how many of these unfortunate souls you are going to adopt?"

"One, for the moment," Gary replied with a sharp laugh. "We'll start with one and see how it goes. They often come with a great deal of physical and emotional needs, and that will have to be considered before we take on another."

"You already have your hands full with Dakota," Roger observed, sipping his beverage and noticing people moving towards the dining area. "Are we sitting inside or on the back?" A couple of long tables had been added to the veranda that ran along the back of the house to accommodate their large numbers this year.

"The evening is fine," Gary agreed to the change in subject. "I'm taking Daks and sitting outside if we're able. Candy is working in the office, so I'm certain she won't be joining us."

"After you," Roger agreed, raising his hand to indicate the direction they should take. As he followed, he added, "I'm glad your family will be growing. Your son deserves a sibling to grow up with."

"Yes," Gary agreed over his shoulder. "I just hope we don't have to wait too long once all the paperwork is complete. There are no guarantees on the time table or what we are going to get when it finally does come through." Spying his wife as he entered the kitchen, he grinned at the burning her small frame produced within him. She had lost a good deal of weight since he first fell in love with her, but it hadn't changed the way he felt in the least. "Our family," he muttered to himself, confident her fears would be put to rest as soon as they laid their new arrival in her arms.

Serving their plates from the buffet that had been spread upon the kitchen table, Gary prepared one for Daks and took it and his own through the back door. Spying the young man kicking leaves, he called, "Daks, you need to get washed, son. I have your plate."

Giggling with his typical glee, the boy left the pile he had been disrupting and scampered into the house. Turning, he entered Lanelle's room where he would be properly groomed and sent out to sit next to his father.

"He seems to be doing well," Gary's closest cousin, Robert, observed as he took the seat across from him.

"Quite well. Having Carol here to mind his instruction at home and the strictness of his school environment has done wonders to improve his skills as well as his manners," Gary supplied. Helping the boy into his seat when he arrived, he cut his meat and presented it to him.

"Where's Candy?" Paula asked as she joined them. "Hasn't she gotten used to us by now? Or is she still hiding somewhere inside?"

"She'll be out, I'm sure," Gary countered, flicking his eyes over at Roger for an instant before he added, "She's still bucking for that straight-A report card, so she's been studying pretty hard for midterms."

"She'll make it," Roger agreed, adding approval to her actions. "She wants us to be proud of her."

"When do you leave for Florida?" Robert asked, certain the trip would take place soon by the coolness of the air.

"We'll fly out on Saturday," the older Ford supplied. "Gary will be delivering us to the airport as usual."

"Absolutely. It's one tradition I hope I always get to keep," Gary lied. Since he and Candy met, he had hated the idea of his parents being so far away over the winter, as getting to them with his new family would prove difficult if the need should arise. However, they were grown adults and capable of deciding to stay home without his nagging if or when they were ready to give up on their seasonal arrangements.

Night fell while the family dined, and as soon as the meal ended, the children all piled out the front door with their bags and plastic pumpkins in hand. Candy came out to see them off, having taken her plate to the office to eat alone while she revised a paper. She felt a little sad that she had missed so much of the gathering, or that she had not been missed by the others as she did so, but it comforted her that her schooling would not last forever.

Watching them go, the group seemed happy to take Daks along, as he had become one of the Ford youngsters in practice, if not by blood. One of Robert and Paula's boys guided him as they cleared the front walk, giving her a wide grin. "You'd never know he wasn't one of them," she observed as Gary joined her at the window to watch.

"He is one of them," he soothed. Sliding his hands over and around her shoulders, he rested his arms above her breasts and hugged her from behind, his chin pressing against the top of her head. "As our new baby will be when it arrives."

Candy stiffened. It had been weeks since she had indulged in thinking about their preparations or the reasons for them. "Of course," she simply agreed, keeping her private fears of what lay ahead to herself. Spying Bella on the couch with a phone in her hand, she winced. The girl reminded her of herself in so many ways, hiding with her distractions and not interacting with the rest of the family unless she were forced to.

"You didn't want to go out with the others?" she asked, pulling herself free and taking a seat next to the girl.

"No. I'm not a child," Bella replied stiffly, not bothering to look up from her glowing device.

Chuckling at her choice of words, Candy exchanged a glance with her husband before standing to leave the girl to her silent scrolling. Pouring wine, they joined the rest of the adults on the back porch, where they were swapping stories and laughing merrily as they had done every year since Candy had known them. Her mother grinning from ear to ear at the head of the table, Candy smiled at the warmth of the people around her despite the difficulty she typically felt at being part of it.

Her mind wandering, she thought about how Bella's attitude had reflected a better-than-thou attitude Candy had sensed from Gary's family since she came into their midst. No matter how hard she tried, she never quite felt right, as if she never would measure up to them or their expectations. Brushing a tear from her cheek, she hoped no one had noticed it in the darkness.

But why would they? They were perfectly content and enthralled with their telling and sharing about things that happened long ago. Things that had not and probably never would include her; not if she could help it. They had seemed to warm to her, but she still wasn't comfortable in their midst. She didn't know how they felt about her deep down and had no intention of finding out.

Giving it a while, she eventually made her excuses and returned to her computer. There, she could hide under the pretense of schoolwork while she avoided contact with the family that would never quite be hers.

THREE

If Wishes Were Horses

SIX WEEKS LATER, time had passed swiftly since Halloween, and the semester had come to an end. The house quiet, Candy sat at her computer alone in the office, pretending to be busy with last-minute work. It was really Gary's office, but these days, she used it more than he did. Staring at the screen, tears streaked her cheeks. Pulling a few tissues from the box on the desk, she dabbed at them before releasing a low, long wail.

Digging at her eyes with the thin material, Candy glared at her grades, which were displayed there on the screen. She had worked so hard. Had wanted it so badly. And yet, here they were: *two Bs, two Cs, and a big fat D.*

She had some decisions to make.

If wishes were horses, then beggars would ride. Her grandmother had used that phrase when she was a kid, before her father was killed and they had drifted apart. She had never quite understood what she had meant by it. But sitting in that chair, the meaning was all too clear.

I can wish all I want. If I don't change something, this is how it's going to be until I graduate... or quit.

The idea of giving up brought on another wave of emotion, and she suppressed the squeal, hoping that neither Carol nor her mother would hear. Angrily clicking to close the box, she stood and left the office. Mounting the stairs unseen, she made it to her bedroom and the sink in the long, narrow lavatory.

Using the cool water, she washed away her sorrow. "No sense crying about it now," she mumbled as she patted her skin with a fluffy hand towel. Her bedroom to the left of her, the door to her right led to the nursery they had constructed out of their spare bedroom; the one she had debated about giving to Daks when Carol came to live with them.

Holding the towel against her face, she breathed through it as she glared at the flat surface that hid the room beyond. Drawn to it, she continued to hold the cloth with her left hand while the right was lowered to find the handle and open the portal.

The room dim, the light from the closed shades was weak on this side of the house. The windows in this room and the one she shared with Gary overlooked the back yard, and the giant trees located there shaded them even further.

Glancing around at the items she had chosen, she sighed. They had kept the room simple, only providing the necessities until they knew for certain the age and sex of the child they would receive, but Gary had insisted on a crib, basinet, and other assorted furniture suitable for a baby.

Baby.

The word frightened her even if she could not bring

herself to explain it to Gary. Bringing a new child into their home had been a big decision, and she still wasn't certain she was ready. Having Dakota had been the most difficult thing she had ever done, and even eight years later, the guilt weighed heavily upon her. *It probably always will.*

Moving to the center of the room, her fingers caressed the rocking chair that her husband had chosen. Made of dark, mahogany-colored wood, a simple green pad provided cushion for the hard seat. Sinking down upon it, she lowered her towel to her lap as she sat stiffly. Her back slowly relaxing against the slats, she closed her eyes and rocked gently back and forth. Just as she breathed out in a long exhale, accepting the quiet calm of the room, a loud and almost shrill jingle interrupted her, jarring her back to reality.

Leaping from the chair, she silenced the device she had left lying next to the sink, then noted it was her husband calling from the station. She hated those calls. Something else she had gotten used to and accepted but wasn't exactly happy about.

"Hello?" she managed as she raised the device to her ear.

"Did I wake you?" Gary asked with a laugh.

"No, you didn't wake me," Candy sniffed, hoping he couldn't hear the sadness in her voice. Her horrible grades would remain a secret for as long as she could hold it.

"Ah, good. We need to meet over at Glenda's."

"Glenda's?" she repeated doubtfully. "I thought we had signed the final documents after the inspection last week."

"Uh, well," he capitulated, sensing she was upset.

Deciding to keep it simple, he explained in short, "She's got a few things we need to go over. Want me to pick you up?"

"No. I'll drive," she sighed. Gary had bought a new car for her over the summer, and for the first time in her life she held a driver's license. He said it would give her freedom, but to her, it felt like more of a burden. "Yes, I'll be there in a bit."

Ending the call, she used the towel once more, then inspected her red-rimmed eyes in the mirror. *Hopefully they'll be normal by the time I get there.*

Tromping down the stairs, her footfalls became almost angry. *Anger is good.* Anger gave her control. She had been fighting against it since she had moved into that house, but if she could hold on to it, she could prevent herself from blubbering the moment she saw him.

She knew he would be there to comfort her if she needed or wanted it. He always was. But sometimes she didn't want to be comforted. *Sometimes I want to stand on my own two feet.*

Donning her jacket against the December air, Candy fluffed her hair, then wrapped her neck with a scarf. Taking her bag and keys, she crossed the yard to the garage and the small blue Toyota she had convinced Gary to choose; a Prius. She liked that it was a hybrid, and therefore better for the environment. She would have preferred the Ford but given their name had decided against it. The recollection of that fact lifted her spirits as she slid into the driver's seat and pushed the button to start it.

Arriving at the agency a few minutes later, Candy felt calmer. She had meditated as she drove, practically ignoring the other cars around her. She knew she would still have to deal with the school situation, but that would wait. She was on Christmas holiday, and for once in her life, she was going to do everything she could to relax and enjoy it. *This year, Christmas is mine.*

Grabbing her bag out of the passenger seat, she threw it over her shoulder and stomped towards the glass doors in the front. The couple had been to Glenda Tucker's office a dozen times by now, and she was familiar with most of it. Whatever new documents they needed to sign shouldn't take long, and she intended to spend the afternoon shopping for gifts for her husband, mother, and son and perhaps even a few for Carol. Anything to take her mind off the dismal report she had been viewing before Gary's call.

As soon as she stepped inside, she could feel the tension in the air. Seated in one of the upholstered chairs in the waiting area, Gary leapt up to meet her. "What's wrong?" she demanded, suddenly afraid he had called her there to tell her they had been denied. It would have crushed him, but she would almost have been relieved. At least that chapter in their lives would have been settled and no longer in limbo as it had been for the better part of a year.

"Hi, kitten," he breathed through a wide grin, pulling her into his arms and hugging her firmly. Inhaling deeply, Gary measured his words. "I didn't want to tell you over the phone."

"Tell me what?" she insisted anxiously, her heart fluttering with anticipation. Freeing herself from his grasp, she looked around to find the receptionist smiling at them broadly. "Oh no," she gasped. Flicking her gaze back to him, she managed, "Baby, what's going on?"

"This way," he replied, taking her hand and leading her into a room they had never seen.

Entering through an ordinary door, the area had been set to look like a house, with a couch along the far wall. Two comfy-looking chairs held the space on the left, and a large, fluffy carpet in the center added a cozy feel to the area.

Toys lined shelves that hugged the wall to the left, and a crib occupied the right-hand side of the entrance. The entire right-side wall was glass, obviously a two-way mirror so that people could hide on the other side and observe whatever took place there.

"Is this some kind of test?" Candy blurted, her raw emotions bubbling beneath the surface.

"No, kitten. All the tests are over." Still holding her fingers, he pulled her gently towards the crib. "I didn't want to look until you got here. I wanted us to see her for the first time together."

"Her," Candy gasped. "Oh my God." Her chest tight, she couldn't breathe. Her feet catching as she dragged them across the carpet, the world moved in slow motion as they reached the edge of the bed, and she stared down at eyes the color of dark chocolate peering up at her.

Standing at the head of the crib, Glenda came into focus for the first time. "Candy. Gary. Allow me to introduce your daughter."

"Dear God," Candy whispered, afraid to move. Afraid to speak. Terrified to touch her. *Sweet Jesus, this is real,* she admitted silently as she noted the car seat they had purchased was tucked under the bed.

Gary wasn't afraid. Reaching eagerly, he lifted the bundle with tears in his eyes and whispering to himself,

"I hoped it would be you." Nodding at Glenda as he placed the infant against his chest, he observed, "I would have thought Joylana would have a happy home by now."

"You know this child?" she gasped.

"Of course," he chuckled, laying her in the crook of his arm and presenting her to his bride. "She was left at the station. I pulled her out of our haven box on Halloween."

"I wasn't aware of that," Ms. Tucker replied, glancing at the pale features of his wife. Swallowing, she confessed, "She had previously been placed. You are correct. However, as you can probably see from her complexion, she is of mixed race. Her previous fosters thought it would not be a problem but have since changed their minds."

"Why us?" Candy asked absently, her fingers trailing a tiny arm as she stared into the soft brown orbs of her new daughter. Regaining her composure, a smile slowly spread across her lips. *This baby is ours.* It was all she could manage, over and over repeating the words to herself and hoping they were true.

Looking down into her calmer expression, Gary offered her the bundle and helped her take possession of their infant. After she had adjusted her against her bosom, he stepped back and beamed at the picture they presented together. Resuming their conversation, he repeated his wife's question, "Yes, why us? I'm sure we aren't next on the list."

"Well, it doesn't exactly work that way," Glenda explained with a shrug. "It's not like a baseball lineup where when it's your turn, you're up," she added with a giggle. Removing the grin, she continued, "You're probably aware that fosters and adoptive parents are predominantly Caucasian. They aren't exactly lining up to offer their homes to children of color, especially those whose background is unknown. Without the medical records of the mother, there is a great deal of uncertainty."

"As we previously discussed," Gary offered, considering the long list of warnings they had been given.

"Yes. But you already have a son with special needs. And you have the financial stability that will cover any medical expenses this child might encounter later in her development." Glenda grew stiff as she finished. "I hope this won't affect your decision."

"No." Gary laughed abruptly, turning to face her. "Joylana will be welcome in our home, and we will give her the best love and care that we can," he reassured.

Glancing at her husband, Candy admired his confidence, as well as the size of his heart. *He's such a good man*, she silently considered. "At least this time, I have a say," she announced with genuine happiness in her voice.

"This time?" Ms. Tucker asked doubtfully.

"I hired our nanny last year without asking her if it was ok," Gary explained with a sheepish grin. "I promised that from now on she would be informed before I brought home any more –" He stopped short, cutting himself off before he referred to Joylana as a stray.

"I get the picture," Glenda replied sharply, raising her chin as she considered his words. "Very well. You may take her, and I will be by for a visit tomorrow. And then another in three days. After that, we will be visiting once a week until further notice."

"To make sure everything is going well," Candy

surmised, still smiling. *How bad could it be?* She had had a baby before, after all. *And this time around, things were going to be different.* At least she hoped that they would be.

"Yes, we want to be sure things are going well, as you put it. This child has already lost her mother and a new home in a very short time. The last thing we want is to uproot her again if we can help it," Glenda explained.

"That's understandable," Gary said calmly. Pulling their infant seat from under the bed, he arranged the blanket and waited for Candy to lay her inside. The moment he snapped the harness into place, a flurry of butterflies went wild within his gut. He hadn't been there for Dakota when he was a baby. No, he had come in late in the game. This time, he was going to be there all the way, and he couldn't wait to take his daughter home and get started on the rest of her life.

FOUR

The Struggle is Real

THE RIDE HOME was filled with a silence the couple rarely shared. Candy had left her car parked at the clinic at Gary's insistence so they each could take part in this experience, and both listened intently to the breath of the baby girl snuggled in her seat. Gary had dutifully strapped it in the center of the bench seat behind them so they both could see her when they stole a peek.

Doing so at one-minute intervals, conflict roiled within Candy. *Am I good enough for this?* Wearing a stoic expression, she only dared to question her abilities silently and gave no outward hint to the conflict within her.

Chewing her bottom lip, she blinked back tears as she recalled the day she had taken Dakota home. He had spent weeks in the hospital following his birth. Although she had visited him daily, she had not been as prepared for the reality of his daily care as she had thought she had been. *Babies need things,* she allowed, swiping at an escaped droplet. Things she hoped she would be able to provide without hesitation.

Sensing her distress, Gerald removed his right hand from the wheel and placed it on the console between them. Wriggling his fingers, he waited for her to take it. When she did so, he sighed with relief. "I know this will be difficult for you. Our daughter will be very different from our son and may have challenges of her own to face."

"I'm sure she will," Candice sniffed. "I'm afraid this will not be as easy as it would seem."

"I'm sure it won't be," he agreed with a small chuckle. "If adopting were easy, no child would ever be in need of a home."

Watching the curb roll past her window, Candy considered that sentiment, then said aloud, "Life is hard. Everyone faces their own set of difficulties." Hers had seemed like a mountain before her that only grew taller no matter how hard she pushed to climb it.

"Yes, we do," he slurred with a grimace. Giving her a final squeeze, he released her digits and reclaimed his hold on the leather cover as he guided the vehicle into their drive and the garage behind.

"Oh," Candy gasped. "We didn't tell mom we were bringing home a baby!"

"Well, you didn't. I spoke to Carol while we waited for you at the clinic, and I let them know Joylana would be joining us for the rest of her life."

His words sent excited spasms rippling through Candy's gut, *the rest of her life* echoing in her ears. "I can't believe this is real."

"Very real," he replied while shutting off the engine. Exiting the vehicle, he climbed into the back seat where he didn't hesitate to unsnap the harness and lift the carrier.

Leaping out her side, Candy followed with short, quick strides. "You sure make a proud papa," she teased, catching them at the back step.

"It's cold," he countered. "I want to get her in and keep her warm."

"And get her out to show her off," she beamed. Her heart thumping inside her chest, she hoped to steal some of his enthusiasm and use it to keep her fears at bay.

As soon as the back door opened, a line formed with three eager faces waiting anxiously to have a look. Glancing at each of them, Candy's cheeks flushed. She hadn't thought to find out what they had been told, and for an instant, she wondered if their new baby would be accepted by everyone in the house. She had agreed to adopting, but it had always felt so long away, as if they had plenty of time for everyone to prepare. Her arrival seemed… sudden.

Holding their new baby as she lifted her from the carrier, things felt surreal, keeping her on edge with mild shots of adrenaline. Cradling her against her chest, she presented her first to Carol for a peek. "Think we can handle this?"

"Without a doubt," the other woman beamed, satisfied with the quick inspection. "I'll get dinner ready while you have a few minutes as a family in the living room."

Shuffling over, Lanelle didn't wait to be asked her opinion, stating loudly, "My, what a handsome set of features!"

"Pretty, mom," Candy laughed, catching a glimpse of Gary's back as he disappeared around the corner in the direction of their office.

"Beautiful," the older woman agreed. "Come and let

me hold her," she insisted as she ambled towards the new chair that had been christened as hers upon its delivery. A fire burned in the hearth nearby, adding a cozy feel to their introduction as she perched on the cushion and patted her lap with her palms, waiting for Joylana to be placed in her arms.

"I see," Dakota joined in at her elbow. Catching the blanket, he pulled it back with his jerky movements, a long "Oh" escaping his pink lips. "So pretty," he observed.

They had told him several times during the renovations that a new baby was coming to live at their house, but Candy had never been certain to what extent he would understand. "Her name is Joylana," she informed her son, her hand smoothing his dark locks as she soothed his excited state.

"Joy'ana," he repeated.

"Wow," Lanelle praised with a grin, "that was close. How about we call her Joy."

"Joy," he tried again. Using a stiff finger, he trailed her scalp and toyed with her dark ringlets. His touch the gentlest he could muster, his grin was unmistakable.

"She's your sister," Gary announced as he rejoined them. Turning to his bride, he continued, "I called and let my parents know of her arrival. Dad was pleased for certain."

"Eve was upset?" Candy replied doubtfully, thinking of any number of reasons her mother-in-law might be unhappy.

"No, but you know my mother." Gary laughed as he took a seat on the ottoman and pressed his palms together to keep them still. "She has a way about her.

She's damned hard to read and never lets on her emotional state if she can help it."

"She didn't say anything negative," Candy pushed, noting Joylana had begun to squirm. "I think we're going to need a bottle."

"No, nothing negative. I'll see that one is being prepared," Gary advised as he stood and trotted into the kitchen. "Were you able to pick up the formula?"

"Of course," Carol chirped. "I have water warmed and ready for the mixing," she informed him, indicating the kettle they had purchased for that purpose.

Combining the warm liquid and the powder they had been instructed to use, he shook the bottle vigorously and observed the milky substance. "It's clumped in the nipple," he grunted. "Next time I'll squeeze it to keep it out of there when I mix it," he added, giving it a few more shakes to complete the job.

Taking his daughter's first meal in their house into the front room, he presented it to Lanelle, who still cradled her against her bosom. Glancing at Candy, he wanted for an instant to snatch the child away so that his wife could do the honors.

Sensing his desire to have her provide the feeding, she shook her head slightly in warning. "Let's let Mimi have the first feeding. Joy seems rather comfortable, and we want her to feel calm her first day here," she offered. "Besides, there will be lots more for us to share."

Agreeing with a sigh, Gary released the bottle and then sat once more to watch as she drank hungrily at the mixture. On the other side of the chair, Daks never left her side, his face flushed with happiness that the new baby who would be sharing his parents had arrived as promised.

Hours later, Candy sat in the rocking chair she had occupied that morning before she received Gary's call. In her arms, she held the baby girl that had appeared in her life so unexpectedly. Listening to the creak of the rungs as she gently swayed back and forth, her mind traced the day in full, from the moment she had pulled up her grades, to standing in Glenda's office staring down at the child they had spent the rest of day taking turns holding.

Even Dakota had gotten two chances to sit on their sofa as she anxiously laid the babe in his arms. However, he had been on his best behavior, and his brown eyes had shone brightly each time he had curled her to his chest. Bouncing her with glee, it was obvious he had understood enough about her presence to feel happiness at her being delivered, and Candy hoped that it would always be so.

"Your car is safely back in the garage, and everything is laid out in the kitchen," Gary announced as he joined her, interrupting her thoughts. "When she wakes us, I'll go down and make the bottle."

"You're quick to volunteer," Candy giggled, aware that late night feedings were not glamorous in the least; she was not really looking forward to that part of their adventure. Clearing her throat, she asked more solemnly, "What did you mean when you told Ms. Tucker that you knew Joy?"

Placing a blanket in the basinet, Gary appeared not to hear her query. "I'm going to put this in next to the bed. Even with the doors open between, I'm afraid we won't hear her, and I want her to be close in case anything happens."

"We'll hear her fine," Candy reassured. "But you can put it in the other room if you like. I'm sure it will be comforting having her close by at the beginning."

"At the beginning," he repeated, pausing his movements to cut her a glare. "What's that supposed to mean?"

"Nothing," she whispered, still staring at the tiny face in her arms. Joy had slept most of the day, but she had opened her dark eyes a few times to inspect whoever was holding her. She had hardly cried at all and seemed content with her new caretakers. "You avoided my question," she pointed out rather than answer his.

"I didn't avoid anything," Gary replied with a scowl. "Someone put Joylana in the baby box at the station on Halloween. I happened to be the one who pulled her out."

"And you didn't think to tell me about it?" Her eyes narrowed into slits, Candice's voice grew deep with inner rage.

"It was Halloween!" He laughed anxiously, aware he probably should have at least mentioned it to her, but he hadn't told anyone, save his father. "We were busy with our guests and you with school, and after that, I guess I forgot. Besides, how was I to know we would eventually bring her into our home?"

"So, tell me about it," Candy urged with a pout, her eyes drawn back to their sleeping charge.

"There isn't much to tell." Gary sighed, taking a seat on the cushion under the window. "She was placed in the box only a few minutes after I arrived at the station. Phil and I pulled her out and inspected her. She seemed fine, and we called the hospital to let them know. While we waited for someone to pick her up, I found a note from her mother asking us to care for her Joylana, and that was it."

"Sounds simple enough." Candy sniffed, her voice giving away the tears she'd been hiding. "I still don't understand how someone could give their baby away."

"Oh, they do far worse than give them away," Gary muttered, returning to his preparations for bed. Carrying the smaller version of the crib into the other room, he returned a moment later. "Anything else we will need during the night?"

"I think we have it all," Candy replied, still upset in a way she couldn't explain. Entering her room through their connected bath, she looked around at the small space, the feel of it completely changed by the tiny bed next to her own. "Do you want to hold her before I put her down?" she asked meekly, offering the bundle to her mate.

Pursing his lips, Gary considered the question. The red rings around his bride's eyes indicated her struggle was real. She had not fallen into the role of Joylana's mother as easily as he had thought she would, and he could tell something bothered her deeply. Maybe several somethings. Accepting the sleeping infant, he grinned despite his misgivings. "Of course I do," he cooed, using a finger on his free hand to caress her cheek. Lifting her to his shoulder, he inhaled deeply, the scent of her fresh skin intoxicating. "I've waited so long to hold something so precious."

Candy's gut turned at his quiet profession, certain he hadn't meant it as a jab, but it had twisted emotions inside her just the same. Climbing under her covers, she tried to ignore the lump in her belly. *Today was a good day,* she told herself for the umpteenth time. Her bad grades were something she would have to deal with, but their baby had arrived, and she should do everything she could not to spoil everyone's happiness, especially that of the man now tucking their baby Joy in next to her.

FIVE

A Girl's Best Friend

WALKING around the kitchen the following morning, Candy bounced her new baby girl in her arms tenderly. The kettle warming, the infant squirmed and whimpered behind the cutest pout she had ever seen.

"Has she actually cried yet?" Caroline asked as she prepared the bottle a few minutes later.

"Yes, in the middle of the night," Candice giggled. "She does have a pair of lungs when she needs them." Catching sight of her husband working his way down the stairs, she left their housekeeper and demanded, "What's that for?"

Basinet in hand, Gary grinned at her, holding back his snarky reply. "I think we need to put her down once in a while," he suggested when the small crib had been reassembled in the living area. "We don't want to spoil her to being held all the time."

That wasn't true, of course. That's exactly what he wanted to do. *Spoil the hell out of her. But as a parent it wouldn't be wise to do so.* He knew he had to be responsible, but the words "as a parent" gave his heart a jolt, and it fluttered with glee at their new addition.

"I guess," Candy muttered, accepting the warm formula and choosing a seat on the right end of the sofa to provide it. Her mahogany orbs open wide, Joylana made small squeaks as she suckled, her tiny fingers splayed against the side of the plastic container as she ate greedily. Tears in her eyes, Candy swallowed, her emotions still oscillating wildly within her.

Watching her, Gary found his bride hard to read. They would be married two full years in a matter of days, but there were still things about his wife he didn't quite understand. She had, after all, agreed to adopting a baby. She had joined in the work and preparations as much as she could, despite her school requirements, and yet…

Gary shook his head vigorously to remove the negative thoughts he could feel forming. Whatever was bothering Candy would work itself out or be revealed in time. Until then, he was much happier focusing on the good stuff, and lately, it was all good stuff in the Ford household. "I'm heading in to the station today," he announced loudly. "I'm going to get everything arranged so I can be off through New Year's if I can swing it."

"That's almost three weeks," Candy observed doubtfully, not breaking the connection between her and Joy. "Do you think you can get that long?"

"I can try," he countered, pulling on his coat. "I'll be back this evening at the latest. Try putting her down once in a while," he commanded, hiding his grin as he turned to leave via the back door.

The bottle empty, Candy placed it on the table next

to her arm. Lifting the babe to her shoulder, she patted her back firmly. "Daddy says I can't hold you all day," she whispered, rubbing the tiny spine when a gasp of air escaped her.

She had just changed her diaper and placed her in the basinet when Daks bounded into the room from the den. "All done with the woowoos?" she asked.

His smile broad, he nodded. Reaching with pudgy fingers, he toyed with the dark hair that clung to her tiny head as he mumbled, "Baby Joy."

"Yes," Candy whispered. "We have to be quiet and still. Baby Joy is sleeping, see?" She indicated the closed eyes as she gently prodded him to leave her alone.

"Wanna hold her," he demanded emphatically, giving the bed a shake and jarring her awake for a brief moment.

"No, Dakota," Candy snapped. Firmly clasping his hands, she pried the one from the side of the crib and pulled the second away from the tiny face. "She isn't a ragdoll to be wagged around." *Yup, this is going to be hard for him to understand,* she mused to herself.

Pulling him over to the couch, Candy lifted him onto her lap and cradled him as she had done the infant. "You're getting too big for this," she teased, still holding him firmly as he squirmed. "My baby Daks is growing up."

"Wanna hold," he insisted, kicking his feet against the cushions.

"Later," Candy insisted, not letting up her grip. She had been in this struggle with him since he was born and knew she couldn't give up. Maybe Gary was right about not holding her all the time. Training a child started early, and she grinned when her rocking won out and Dakota calmed down and relaxed against her chest.

His fingers toying with her hair, he sighed loudly. He was still typically non-verbal, only speaking in small spurts, but his emotions had grown more stable in the three years they had lived in that house. He obviously wasn't happy at being told *no*, but he was far more accepting of the redirection than he might have been in years past.

Happy to have averted the tantrum, Candy advised quietly, "When Joy wakes up, I'll call you in, and you can have a few minutes with her. Will that be ok?"

Daks nodded, pushing himself up to sit on her lap. "Pretty momma," he cooed, his fingers tracing the curve of her jaw.

Her heart melting, Candy grinned. "Thank you, baby. Go play in the den and let Joylana sleep. Or you can go outside for a bit if you want."

Pushing himself off her legs, Dakota scampered into the kitchen where Lanelle sat in her favorite chair next to the door of her room. She had been observing how well her daughter handled the situation with pride in her aged eyes.

"Mimi outside," Daks announced, grasping her hand and giving her a pull to stand. Content to be his playmate for a few hours, Lanelle obliged, and they donned their coats before they exited the back door and made a beeline for the swings.

"I'll get it," Candy called to the rest of the house when their front bell rang. Opening the portal, she forced a smile at her best friend.

"Surprise!" Cathy sang, holding up what appeared to be a trashcan in her hands.

"Uh, thanks," Candice laughed, stepping back to allow her inside and quickly closing the door behind her. "I didn't know you were coming."

"Well, it wouldn't have been a surprise if I had called, now would it," her friend countered as she placed the pink tub on the coffee table that ran along the front of the sofa.

"That's true," the shorter girl sighed. Glancing over into the diaper pail, she could see a stockpile of baby paraphernalia inside. "What's all this? We already have half this stuff upstairs."

"You can never have too many baby supplies," her friend teased. "I just wanted to make sure you had everything covered." Leaning over the crib, she gasped, "She's so dark."

"She's mixed," Candy replied quietly, biting her bottom lip.

"Mixed?"

"Yeah. Black for sure. And something else. Maybe two something else," she explained.

"Oh," Cathy nodded. "Well, she's beautiful either way."

"Of course she is," Carol inserted, joining the pair with a tray of cups and a pot of hot cider. Placing the spread on the table next to the gift, she scowled. "Do you think that will be everyone's reaction when they first see her?"

Blinking rapidly, Candy sighed, "I certainly hope

not. I didn't mention it on my post. I just said we had brought home our new baby. My page is private, so only a handful of people will see it anyway. I guess that's how you knew," she deduced as she eyed their visitor.

"Yup. I saw and went shopping as any sensible woman would." Cathy laughed as she pulled at the blankets to unwrap the infant. "You don't mind if I hold her," she added, not really asking for permission as she lifted the tiny body and curled it into the crook of her arm. Taking Lanelle's chair and propping her feet on the ottoman, she cooed, "Oh, Candy. You are so lucky."

Cathy didn't have any children and had no plans for any in the near future. With only one semester left at the Junior College, she would be moving on to a four-year school soon enough, followed by a new career to settle into before she could even think about a family.

Candy sometimes felt jealous of Cathy's freedom and the way her life seemed so well planned and orderly. *Not like the chaos mine has always been,* she silently observed. Aloud, she countered, "If you say so."

"I do say so," Cathy replied, her tone growing somber. "I plan to have my own someday, but I can't help but fear it might not ever happen."

Glancing between them, Carol could feel their spirits dipping. "Hey, have a seat and let's enjoy a warm drink with our new arrival. Leave all the doubts at the door."

"Yes ma'am," Candy grinned sheepishly. Accepting her cup, she curled into her seat on the sofa, tucking her stocking feet beneath her. Secretly glad her friend had come for the visit, she felt relief that Cathy had been accepting of her new charge. "I'm sure you will have a family of your own one day," she stated confidently.

"Both of you," she added, cutting her eyes back and forth between her two best friends as she enjoyed a sip of the hot beverage.

Candy didn't have much in the way of friends before she met Gary, but she and Cathy had become inseparable over the past few years, not to mention all that Carol had been there for. Cathy's reaction to most everything she did was important to her, and it meant a great deal that no matter what happened, she could at least count on her two besties to be there to the bitter end.

The trio was still enjoying their afternoon when the doorbell rang yet again.

"Who can that be?" Caroline asked as she stood to answer it.

"Glenda," Candy replied with a sigh. She had forgotten about their agent's intent to visit. "She'll be stopping by frequently until we have been cleared to adopt Joy, so you might as well get used to it."

"Or give her a key," Cathy joked. Still holding the slumbering infant, she grunted, "Should I put her down?"

"Not at all. Aunt Cathy is allowed to visit," Candice teased with a genuine grin. Standing to greet their advocate, she held the expression and hoped that she passed for calm as their housekeeper closed the door behind her. "Sorry. I forgot you were coming."

"No need to apologize," Glenda countered smoothly, her eyes taking in the disarray of their ordinarily pristine home. She had wondered how Joylana's arrival in their midst would affect their everyday life, and it was clear she had put them into the typical chaos most families overcame in a few days to weeks. Giving Cathy a cursory glance, she questioned doubtfully, “Is this a relative?”

“No, this is my best friend and school mate, Catherine Douglas.” Candy kept the explanation short, not feeling there should be anything wrong with having a friend over.

“I see,” Ms. Tucker replied evenly. “I’ll only be a moment.” Taking the stairs, she made her inspection of the child’s designated room, noting it appeared to be clean and organized. Coming back down the stairs, she smiled despite her fears, as it would seem everything was in order. Taking a right into the kitchen, she had a look around in there as well before rejoining the others.

“Satisfied?” Candy clipped with a sniff.

“Yes.” Leaning over, Glenda peered down at the sleeping babe. “If you don’t mind, I need you to unwrap her.”

“Unwrap her!” Cathy gasped. “What on Earth for?”

“I’m here for a safety check. The house looks fine, but I also need to inspect the child.”

Candy’s face flushed in an instant, her heart pounding against her ribs. Stomping across the few steps between them, she practically snatched her daughter away.

Placing her in the basinet, she unfurled the blanket that kept her snug, and Joy stretched into the freedom. “Carol, would you mind preparing a bottle? It will be time to eat soon, and I’m sure being disturbed will speed process.”

Pursing her lips, Glenda chirped, “You know this is necessary. We have to ensure the safety of those in foster care.”

“No doubt,” Candy hissed, not certain what made

her angrier, that Joy had been disturbed by the visit or that someone might think she or Gary was capable of harming her.

Making the inspection quick, the social worker observed gruffly, “She appears fine. I’ll be back in a few days for another visit. I can let myself out,” she added at the end as she reached the door.

“We’ll be here,” Candy called after her, barely getting the reply out before the latch closed behind her.

On her feet, Cathy reached for her friend’s arm. Giving it a firm squeeze, she reassured, “I bet they do that to everyone. Like she said, they can’t be too careful.”

“We’ve been through enough background checks and screenings. They should know we would never hurt her.” Bending over the crib, Candy retucked the blanket and lifted Joy with trembling hands.

“Don’t let it bother you,” Carol seconded as she returned with a warmed bottle in hand.

Accepting the formula, Candy sank onto her spot on the couch and began the feeding without bothering to argue. They would be under scrutiny for months, and she had to play the game if they had any hope of the final adoption taking place.

However, as she watched the tiny mouth pull at the nipple, she couldn’t shake the gnawing in her gut that something could go wrong.

Anything in fact, and it could mean in the end they would not be allowed to keep her, and that scared her much worse than her fear that they would.

SIX

An Ordinary Day

THE FOLLOWING MORNING, Gary and Candy slept late, allowing Joy to wake them rather than the alarm. Gary had been successful in securing some time off, as Tom was ready to take over the station at a moment's notice. He would be running things until the second of January when Gary would return.

Lying in the still of the morning, Gerald Ford listened to the rhythmical breathing of his wife and daughter. As they slept, he tried his last name on their new family member. *Joylana Ford. Joy Ford.* It had a nice ring to it, he had to admit. *Ut oh.*

Whimpers had begun to float across the room, but before he could move, Candy had thrown back the covers and scooped up the infant. "You could have let her wake up a little more," he teased as she wrapped the blanket and prepared to take her downstairs for feeding.

"I don't like to let them cry," Candy confessed with a small grin. "I was told it was good for them when Dakota was a baby, but the sound gets on my nerves and quickly. I'd rather not."

"It's ok," Gary agreed, pushing the comforter back as well and preparing to stand. "Let's take her out with us today. We'll do a little shopping. Maybe go to Walmart if it's not too crowded. The supercenter would have almost everything we could want at this point." Being a weekday, it wouldn't be as bad as a Saturday or Sunday, but with little more than a week before Christmas, it would be worse than usual.

"We'll see," his wife replied noncommittally. Leaving Gary to finish his morning routine, Candy made her way downstairs, still in her pajamas and bath robe. Her soft slippers made scuffing noises as she shuffled around the kitchen to prepare the water and powder mix, and she grinned at the noise.

In her arms, Joy twisted her tiny fist, sucking on it from different angles as she became more frustrated at the wait. Reaching her breaking point, her whimper built to a loud squawk as Lanelle appeared in the door of her bedroom, which lay off the kitchen on the other side of the long table.

"Well, looks like she's making herself at home," the older woman observed.

"Rightly so," Candice shot back, skillfully making the bottle with one hand while bouncing the crying bundle with the other arm. The nipple in place, she gave her mother a satisfied grin as she silenced the loud wails with the device. Hungry slurps replaced the cries, and Candy giggled. "I guess I haven't lost my touch."

"Mothering is an instinct," Lanelle agreed. "Once we perfect it, we never forget how."

Gary grinned to himself, catching his mother-in-law's words just before he entered the room. "How about dads? Do we get some instincts as well?"

"Of course," his mother-in-law teased. "Although, I think yours were well developed long before you finally got your family to use them on."

"Indeed," he agreed, helping himself to a cup of coffee. Leaning over his wife, who had claimed a seat at the table, he watched as their baby suckled. "They only require such care for a short amount of time."

"Hah!" Candy snorted. "I told you it all seems great in the beginning, but over time, it's not nearly as much fun."

"You seem cynical." Gary frowned, pouring a cup of the brew for his bride. Running fingers through his shower-fresh locks, he placed the offering before her. "Perhaps it will be different this time, since Joy isn't…" His voice trailed away as he decided not to articulate exactly how Joylana would be unlike Dakota. "I'm sure you get the picture," he said instead.

"I get the picture." His wife sighed, not looking at him for fear he would see the guilt she felt at almost every moment in her eyes. "If we are going to Walmart, we should do it quickly. It will get crowded in the afternoon, when the schools let out."

"Right. Perhaps I should take over the feeding, and you can get dressed," he offered, holding out open palms for emphasis. He had already completed his primping and donned suitable attire for an outing.

Placing the baby in his waiting arms, Candy glanced up to see the grin on his handsome features. He was right. This time was nothing like when Dakota had been born, but she could not stop comparing the two of them. What happened to her son was her fault even if no one else blamed her. Having Joy around only brought her old feelings of guilt to the surface, but if she were careful, at least she could keep them hidden and tucked safely out of the way. "I won't be long," she offered with a smile of her own.

Stomping up the stairs, she gave herself a pep talk, hoping she would relish the day with her husband and their new baby. *After all, we've waited almost a year for her arrival. We might as well enjoy every minute of it now that she's here.*

"Not too bad," Gary observed as they pulled into the parking lot in front of the long, tan building. This time of year, the spaces were often filled to the very edges, but at barely ten a.m., more than half the lot remained empty.

"It won't be this way for long," Candy countered as he selected a spot close to the door. In the seat behind them, Joy slept comfortably, and they had a bottle for her in the bag of diapers she had packed, along with a change of clothes. "This is our first time out with her," she observed with a small grin.

"One of many," Gary added as he opened the back door and lifted out the carrier. Catching a whiff of wind, he paused to tuck the blankets in around Joy's small body, ensuring she would remain undisturbed by the frigid gusts.

Taking the north entrance, they had the pharmacy on their left as they entered. Gary squinted at the bright yellow Subway sign on the far side of the store, past the registers. He and Candy had shared their first meal together there, and although it hadn't been a real date, he had cherished it all the same. "We should have lunch while we're here," he observed.

"Feeling sentimental?" Candy teased. Working a basket back and forth to get it out of the corral, she held it while he placed Joy's carrier in the bottom. Reaching over, she adjusted the blanket so she could see the tiny round face of the sleeping infant. Admiring the dark contrast of her flesh against the pale white of her own, she smiled. *Joy is more than a baby. She's a little person. An individual.* Candy couldn't wait for her to grow and present herself and her personality to the world.

"Gary?"

A loud male voice interrupted Candy's thoughts. Pulling her eyes away from her daughter, she noted her husband shaking hands with a distinguished-looking gentleman dressed in a suit and long black coat. *He's a bit overdressed for Walmart,* she mused. Smiling as she was introduced, she offered her own hand.

"Candy, this is Paul Snyder," Gary informed her with a nod at the older man. "He's one of our affiliates with the company."

Glancing at the basket, Paul only appeared to be half listening as he examined the tiny features in the cart.

"This is our new baby," Candy stated crisply, sensing the judgement in his demeanor.

Shifting his doubtful gaze to the couple, Mr. Snyder's expression had grown tense, his smile strained as his eyes darted between them. He wanted an explanation but not badly enough to ask for one. If Gary had decided to pretend the child belonged to him, that was none of his business after all. "Well, Merry Christmas," he said instead, giving them a firm nod before he turned on his heel and exited the store without another word.

"Wow, that was a bit awkward," Candy breathed, her eyes wide as she stared after the stuck-up man.

"Yeah," Gary coughed, glancing at Joy. "Perhaps we should have mentioned she is adopted."

"You don't think –" Candy began, cutting herself off before she accused the stranger of anything sinister.

"He could just be in a hurry," Gary half-heartedly agreed, secretly afraid of what the real reason could have been. Pushing the cart in front of him, he led the way to the infant section instead, where they intended to stock up on more necessities now that they knew more about their long-awaited arrival.

Candy wandered slowly through the racks, picking out clothing, blankets, and decorations for Joys sparse nursery. When Daks had been born, money had been tight, and hardship had hounded them for years. Now their lives were settled, and their means far outweighed their needs. "You don't mind if I splurge a little?" she asked a little breathlessly, her excitement surfacing for the moment.

"Splurge away," Gary suggested, happy to see her smile appeared unstrained and genuine. Removing his coat, he got comfortable, allowing his wife all the time she needed to get into the spirit of the holiday and their new baby. Pulling the blankets aside and unstrapping the bundle inside, he lifted Joy to his shoulder. He managed the cart with one hand, then used it to pat the infant gently each time they stopped.

Her tiny head uncovered, Joylana rested it against the warmth of his shirt. Her fist finding her mouth, she sucked noisily near his ear, occasionally opening her eyes to have a look around. His giant hands gentle as they patted and smoothed her small frame, Gary was in a heaven he never could have imagined.

Around them, other shoppers noticed the couple and their small charge. Glances and whispers abounded, with the occasional stiff digit and hard stare. Eventually, Gary became aware of the attention they were drawing, only then realizing Candy had also become aware. Sidling up to her, he asked quietly, "Are you ok, kitten?"

"Yes. Why wouldn't I be?" she replied, holding her head down and observing an elderly couple who were obviously in deep conversation.

Sliding Joy down from his shoulder, Gary cradled her against his broad chest. Planting a gentle kiss atop her crown, he grinned. "I can't believe how passive she is. I'd heard babies cried all the time, but she's given hardly a whimper since her arrival."

"It's all in their nature." Candy's reply seemed stiff, and she dropped a few more items in their cart before pushing her fingers through the wire end and pulling it after her as she left the baby department. "I need to get Daks a few more things for Santa to deliver, and we can get out of here."

"Out of here," he repeated, trailing behind her, to the right of the cart. They passed more fellow shoppers, and he noted often that their eyes trailed him for as long as they could, and a few even doubled back for a second look. "You'd think these people had never seen a baby before," he muttered when they arrived on the toy truck aisle.

"I'm sure that's not what's causing it," Candy blurted with a scowl. She might have given Paul Snyder the benefit of the doubt, but half an hour and a hundred people later, she feared one of them would involve security or the police at any moment.

Choosing a few new items to add to Daks's collection, Candy turned to face her husband and assess their situation. When their eyes met, he simply gave her a shrug and a half smile.

Seeing his indifference to their undue attention, she again caught the cart and headed for the checkout. Her mind racing, her thoughts traced the years ahead of them as Joylana grew. Scenarios where a white woman with a black child would draw attention. *Every day of our lives,* she mused. *No wonder the first couple had given her back.*

Candy wasn't sure if knowing someone else had backed out should be a warning or a reason to push even harder. All she knew was that having people stare at her in their questioning and even accusing manners did not sit well with her. By the time they stood in front of the cashier, her happiness at the outing had vaporized, and an empty disappointment rested in the pit of her gut.

SEVEN

Skin Deep

GARY LOADED their bags and a few boxes in the back of his Suburban while Candy placed Joy into her carrier and snapped her safely into the back seat. He could tell by the droop of his wife's shoulders that she had been upset by their reception, and they were in for a long drive home.

Deciding to let her cool off for a moment, he climbed behind the wheel, starting the engine and giving it a few minutes before he backed out of the spot and crept towards the street. "Wow, the lots near full. I didn't realize how long we were in there."

No reply. Instead, Candy sat staring stiffly out the front window, her hands folded in her lap. Her lips drawn into a thin straight line, displeasure radiated from her.

"I'm sure it will get easier," he tried again, sad that she had let the strangers steal her happiness in the moment. "We'll get used to having her around and to the way people react, just as we are with Daks. It will be second nature." He made the excuse, hoping she let the dark mood go.

Glaring at the traffic, Candy could feel the frown pressing against her forehead, the crinkle of skin heavy above her left eye. Next to her, Gary appeared calm, as if nothing had happened while they were in the store. Stealing concerned glances at him, Candy didn't have the words to explain the depth of her fears or her anger.

Lashing out at her husband, she bit at him with a sharp tongue, "I doubt we will ever get used to having strangers looking down on us. At least I hope we don't."

Not saying a word, Gary reached over to her lap, where her hands were gripping each other tightly. Using nimble fingers, he pried them apart and folded his right hand around her left, pulling it to the console between them.

"That's it?" she mocked him openly. "Nothing to say?"

"What can I say, kitten? I know this hurt of yours runs deep. I've always known it."

"Oh, so now this is my hurt. These people with their stares and questioning eyes are somehow my fault."

"It's no one's fault. And it isn't our problem to fix." The words sounded odd coming from him, the man who was always fixing problems, especially for other people.

"It doesn't bother you that your business buddy thinks your wife is a whore? That I got knocked up by some other man, obvious to anyone with eyes to see the color of Joy's skin. You should have told him we were adopting her."

"Is that what we should do? Always starting every conversation by explaining away their judgments before they can make them? I told you this isn't our problem. It's theirs. If they are bigoted assholes, they aren't our buddies, and Paul can go fuck himself if he's got any such notions he needs to have explained." Antagonism not his best side, Gary took a side step and tried for humor. "How about matching T-shirts with some catchy slogan? *She's adopted, so it's ok that she's black.*"

"That's not funny, Gary," Candy bit back angrily. Glancing at their slumbering passenger, she winced. "It's always going to be like this. People staring and wondering."

"And making up crazy stories when we don't come out and explain right away. Yeah, it's always going to be this way. But it's their problem, kitten. Not ours. Joy is our daughter, and we don't have to explain anything to them." Giving her hand a squeeze, he swallowed firmly. Forcing calm into his tone, he said more gently, "I know how you always want things to be perfect, but I would hope by now you realize it's ok even when it's not."

"What do you mean I always want things to be perfect?" she growled in return.

Silence. How could he say any more without hurting her? Candy, who was obsessed with the oddest, most insignificant things. She was his princess. His queen. But her father had died too early in her life to make her understand her importance in the world. That, or he hadn't taken the time before he left her. His thoughts turning, Gary knew he would never let that happen to his daughter.

Not getting a response, Candy's blood boiled. "Nothing to say? That's fine. You can think whatever you like about me, because I know I'm not perfect." Her voice quavered, thinking of her grades and how hard she had worked to no avail. "You who are always out to rescue everyone. You want to work on someone? Why don't you work on that?"

The vehicle coming to an abrupt halt at a red light, Gary's head pivoted, and his gaze snapped to meet hers. "I'm a fireman. It's my job to rescue people."

"Exactly," she clipped. "You picked that job because you were drawn to it. You rescued me and my son, and now you want to do the same for Joylana. Not because of who she is, but because of who she isn't."

"What's that supposed to mean?" he demanded, his eyes narrowing slightly at the presumed insult.

"Nothing," she coughed, a horn sounding behind and alerting him to the traffic that had begun to move again.

Putting his attention back on the road, he held her fingers firmly, rubbing against them with his thumb. He refused to pull his hand away despite how much her words had hurt him. He was a rescuer and always had been. As a boy, he was the first to bring the ladder if a cat ever got caught in a tree, but that didn't mean he had chosen his bride in an attempt to rescue her. *Cat. Kitten. Well, crap.* He had never looked at it that way.

Over his shoulder, Joy squirmed in her carrier, a low moan filling the Suburban's tense quiet. "It's ok, precious," he soothed, glancing in the mirror, then around at the other cars filling the street and dragging down their pace. "We'll be home soon, and momma'll get you a nice warm bottle."

His words were hardly spoken when she broke into an actual wail. Candy clenched her fists at the shrill sound, her nails digging into his flesh. Gary could feel the tension mounting in her stiff form, as if she felt physical pain at the sound. "Does it bother you that much? She's crying, but she'll be fine."

"Yes, it hurts that much." Candice sniffed, her eyes fixed on the window next to her to hide her tears. If she had been the one driving, she would have pulled over and stopped to offer the feeding right then just to restore the peace. "I can't believe you let them think such horrible things about me or you. He must have thought you are an idiot, either to believe she could be yours or to stay with me after I had betrayed you in such a way."

Realizing she was still stuck on what had happened at the store, he grinned then broke into an actual laugh. Turning on his blinker, he changed lanes and pulled into a small coffee shop. "Come on, kitten. Our Joy needs rescuing," he teased as he unfastened his seatbelt and climbed out to retrieve her.

Her cries coming as loud screams, he placed the carrier on the table and retrieved the bottle of water from the bag. Carrying it over to the counter, he asked politely, "Would you have any way of warming this? We'd like to feed our baby while we have a hot drink for ourselves."

"Sure," the clerk replied, taking the bottle and pouring the liquid into one of their clean metal cups. Applying the steam-wand, it only took a few seconds to bring up the temperature and pour it back, handing it over.

"Thanks." Gary accepted the bottle and returned to his wife to add the powdered formula and give it a few shakes.

Holding Joylana in her arms, Candy did her best to comfort her. Feeling the eyes of the other patrons upon them, a warm flush crept up from her chest, staining her neck and cheeks. Looking up when he presented the meal, their eyes met. The warmth of his mahogany orbs calmed her, drawing her in and wrapping her in their safety.

"Would you like coffee or hot tea?" he asked gently once she had taken a seat and the feeding had commenced.

"Hot chocolate, please," she replied with a shy grin. No matter how badly things were going, Gary was always her rock, and suddenly those around them didn't matter. She and her husband rarely argued, and she was glad this fight had been a mild one.

Leaving her, Gary ordered their drinks, then returned to the small table where his wife sat in one of the stiff-backed chairs, rocking gently back and forth as she hummed to the suckling infant. Claiming the one across from her, he caught the gaze of an old man who appeared displeased by the scene. "Hi," Gary offered with a grin and a firm nod at the old geezer, who immediately pursed his lips and looked away.

"She'll need a change as well," Candy informed him once he had pulled his chair around the table to sit closer to them.

"I'm sure they have a changing table in both the bathrooms," he observed. "Most places do these days."

"Yes, thank God." Candy chuckled. "They were a new thing when Dakota was a baby, so it was hit or miss whether or not you would find one."

"Hmm."

Grinning at the non-reply, Candy accepted her cup

of warm liquid. Taking a noisy sip, she could feel her spirits lifting. Turning her attention to the child in her arms, she admired the dark eyes that were firmly fixed on her face as she drank eagerly from the bottle, her flushed cheek still damp from her tears.

"Thank you for stopping. Joylana doesn't deserve to be left to cry so early in her life."

"And thank you for being such a wonderful and caring mom," he replied, using his cup to hide his full grin. "It's ok that you aren't perfect. We all love you anyway."

Her thoughts wandering, Candy contemplated her terrible grades. Licking her lips, she asked in a hushed voice, "What would you say if I decided to take a semester off?"

His mouth falling open, Gary gaped at her. "A semester off. I had no idea you were even considering such a thing." Subconsciously, his eyes flicked down at the babe in her arms and almost instantly back to his bride's. "Is it because of Joy?"

"Mostly, yes. Carol is a great nanny, but she's not her mother. I can go to school any time, but Joylana will only be a baby once. I don't want to miss it." Tears filled her eyes, the stress of their seemingly ordinary day pushing them over the edge and sending them streaming down her cheeks. "I want to be there for her," she whispered. "If I had been pregnant, we could have made our plans firm, but like this…" She paused, dabbing at the droplets, then added in a shaky voice, "It all feels so uncertain."

"Oh, honey," Gary cooed. "You take all the time you need. You are exactly right. School will be there when you are ready to go back." The words ringing in his ears, he swallowed his fears. If Candy decided to quit and be a full-time mother, that was her choice to make. They didn't need her earning potential and never had. He had only encouraged her because he thought it was what she wanted.

"I'm going to think about it," Candy muttered. Wiping at her flushed cheeks, she noticed the bottle had been drained, and her baby appeared calm and relaxed. Placing the empty on the table, she lifted Joy to her shoulder where she could give her gentle bounces and rubs to encourage the belch that would follow.

Once the task had been accomplished, she hoisted the diaper bag and made her way to the restroom in the back. While she was gone, Gary leaned back in his chair and drank calmly from his lukewarm brew.

"You know that baby isn't yours," the old man next to him sneered.

"Pardon?" Gary coughed, sitting up straight to glare at him. Anger burned in his chest, and for a moment he thought about decking the guy.

"That kid. The niglet."

Candy returned just in time to hear the word fall from the crinkled lips and to prevent her husband from crushing his skull with the mug in his hand. "Baby, I think it's time to go," she said simply while laying Joylana in her carrier and fastening the strap.

"Yeah, time to go," he repeated as if in a trance. His eyes fixed on the other patron, Gary watched as he drank calmly from his cup as if he had never said a word.

Still fuming when they arrived at their SUV and everyone had been securely fastened in, he started the vehicle and then paused, his hands gripping the wheel.

"Thank you for getting me out of there. For a second, all I wanted to do was knock that guy on his ass."

"Exactly," Candy clipped. "Now you know why I was so upset about your friend, Snyder or whatever his name is."

"Paul Snyder," Gary provided with a grimace. "I can't believe he called her that."

"Well, you might as well get used to it, especially from old people," Candice warned. "If she's going to be ours, we'll be the ones to defend her when idiots say such things or dry her tears when they hurt her feelings with such nonsense."

"If," Gary stated flatly. "What do you mean *if*? We're going to be her parents, Candy. We already are."

Blinking at him, her eyes grew wide. She hadn't put her fears into words, at least not on purpose, but they had slipped out when she least expected it. "I'm sorry," she whispered. "I didn't mean it that way."

"And in what way did you mean it?" he demanded loudly, noticing the old man shuffling out of the store and climbing into an older-model car. "I can't believe that thing still runs," he observed under his breath.

Hearing the words, Candy snickered. When her laugh grew loud, she held her gut but kept rolling.

"What's so funny?" he demanded crossly.

"For a second I thought you were talking about the old man. He's got to be close to a hundred in his decrepit state."

"I doubt that," Gary snickered, her joviality lifting his dark mood. "Ninety, maybe. Old bastard should watch his mouth."

"There you go again, my rescuer," Candy breathed, calming her inhalations. Placing her hand on the side of his seat, she reached for his hair and teased the nape of his neck with agile digits.

"Yeah, a real knight in shining armor," he mused. "What did you mean by if?" he redirected her back to the previous question.

"I'm afraid something will happen, and they won't let us keep her," Candy confessed. "I don't know if I could take it if that were to happen."

The old car out of sight, Gary turned his attention back to his wife. "Is that what's been bothering you? You're scared to love her, or to make any real commitments, in case they take her away?"

Swallowing, Candy shrugged. She had lost so much in her life that it was hard to explain how deeply she dreaded even the thought of losing someone else.

"Someday we're going to get this figured out." He chuckled as he backed out of the spot and pulled up to the exit.

"What?"

"Me the rescuer and you with your perfectionistic tendencies."

"And how do you propose we do that?" she demanded, the scowl threatening to return to her delicate features.

"I'll stop trying to save everyone. That'll be my part," he mused. "And you," he pondered, his eyes taking on a distant look before he glanced at her. "You need to let go of the fear and be happy in the here and now. Stop worrying about how things are going to be tomorrow or next year. Just… be good with today. Enjoy it a little."

His words shocked her, and she inhaled deeply as she prepared her rebuttal, but Joylana sighed the sweetest of coos at that moment, giving her pause. Holding her breath, Candy listened to her daughter breathe, the sweetness of her sounds calling to her. "Today," she stated softly. "Yeah, I think I can handle that." Or at least she would give it her best effort to.

EIGHT

Family Matters

"I'LL GET IT," Candy called to the rest of the house. She had been standing over the basinet in the living room and watching Joylana sleep when the chimes sounded.

Reaching the front door, she peeked through the eye-hole to see a few of Gary's family members waiting on the other side. *What the heck?* she grunted to herself in surprise as she swung the portal wide. "Annette. Bella. What a pleasant surprise!" she lied. "Quick, come in, and let's shut out the cold."

Entering quickly as instructed, the cousins tumbled inside, presenting a small gift bag each. "Eveline says your adoption has arrived sooner than expected," Annette explained as soon as the door was closed behind her.

"Yes, we've only had her a couple of days," Candice agreed with a faint grin, feeling a little guilty that it had been left to her mother-in-law to spread their happy news.

Dropping her bag on the table, Bella stepped over to

the baby's bed and glared at the small, sleeping form. "Why's she so dark?"

"Bella, don't be rude," her mother rebuked. Also staring at Joy's face and hands, she waited for the explanation, almost certain they had not been given a white child. Such an occurrence had not even crossed her mind when she heard that Gary and Candy intended to adopt. Swallowing, she soothed, "Babies come in all kinds, Bell. I'm sure your cousin will be loved despite the tint of her skin."

"Tint," Candice scoffed under her breath, the word grating on her nerves. She had heard enough hurtful remarks in a single day to last her a lifetime, and their journey had only just begun.

Catching the hiss of her words, Annette held up her hands. "Sorry, no offense. I'm just not sure what to say! I'm surprised. That's all. Eve didn't warn us, you see." Looking thoughtful, her lips pursed into a perfect "O" before she added cautiously, "I wonder if she is even aware."

Her eyes narrowing, Candy could hear Gary coming down the stairs. Her mind leaping to their outing that morning and their public reception, she sighed. "Yes, I suppose everyone will be caught off guard. I didn't speak to her, so I have no idea if she knows or not or simply chose not to say. But surely Gary mentioned it." A frown dented her forehead as she considered whether the color of Joy's flesh would matter to the rest of the Fords. Strangers were one thing, but family… Family mattered. It would break her heart if she weren't accepted by her new kin.

"Can I hold her?" Bella asked, drawing the conversation away from the edge of argument.

"I don't see why not," Gary agreed eagerly as he arrived next to his wife, only catching the tail end of their conversation. "Can you lift her, or do you want to sit, and I'll place her in your arms like we do for Daks?"

"I'm not a child," Bella growled, reaching to remove the blankets and scooping up the doll-like form.

"Watch her head," Candy suggested, moving as if to help her, then noting the girl appeared quite adept at holding an infant. "You seem familiar with baby handling," she observed with a giggle.

"The cousins on Dad's side of the family are all younger than me," the girl explained. "I'm the oldest, with only one even close to my age." When Joy had been curled into the crook of her arm, Bella began to bounce slightly at the knee. Joy had opened her eyes at the transition but slowly closed them and resumed her nap virtually undisturbed. "She's so peaceful," their young visitor observed.

"Yes," Candy agreed. "She's been quiet compared to Daks at that age. He was a handful from the moment he was born." Candice watched the girl in surprise, she and her mother both friendlier in the smaller setting, thankfully. *Maybe we'll get to be friends after all,* she mused.

Twisting, Bella took a seat on the edge of the sofa, her bouncing converted to rocking back and forth. A smile crept onto her features, indeed a sharp contrast after her dark mood at the family gathering only a few weeks before. Lifting a small hand, she admired the slender digits and observed aloud, "I like the darkness of her skin. Creamy, like dark coffee."

"Bella," her mother sighed.

"It's ok," Candy sniffed. "We might as well get used

to it. I mean, people do the same thing with Dakota, so why should Joy be any different?"

"The same thing?" Annette asked with a doubtful scowl, obviously disturbed at their lack of social grace during their current visit.

"Oh, you know." Candy wafted a hand at the rest of the furniture and exhaled loudly as she offered her a seat. "People say things, often speaking before they consider how it might sound on the receiving end. They don't mean any harm, they just don't know any better."

Accepting a place on the couch next to her daughter, Annette relaxed for the first time since meeting Candy. "I understand. When Bella was little, we would get the same inconsiderate questions. *'When's the boy coming?'* or *'Still trying for a junior?'* Things like that were often asked without a second thought." Laying her hand on her daughter's shoulders, she ran her palm down the arch of her back.

"Ha!" Lanelle coughed as she and Daks joined the group. Taking her customary chair, she beamed, "It's always like that. With Candy, though, it all changed when her father passed. *'How do you manage?'*" the older woman mocked, earning a few surprised glances and anxious giggles. She hadn't managed and had fallen into alcoholism, leaving Candy unsupervised for much of the time. Realizing she had led them to an awkward silence, she folded her hands in her lap and waited.

"It's ok, mom," Candy soothed as she lifted Dakota onto her lap. "We all make mistakes and have times we wish we could take back what we've said." Holding her son firmly by crossing her arms around him, she added more quietly, "Sweet brother, letting cousin Bella hold our baby Joy."

Unsmiling, the boy never took his eyes off the two girls. Studying them intently, he appeared to be considering what he should do about the situation and ready to intervene if his new sister needed protection of any kind.

Glancing around at the gathering of women, Gary cleared his throat, then announced, “It would appear that I’m out numbered. I think I’ll go help in the kitchen and get ready for the feeding that will be coming up shortly.”

Watching him go, Candy smiled fully. “Ford men are the best,” she mumbled, recalling that Roger held the same caring attitude. “I hope Dakota learns by their example.”

“They are indeed,” Annette agreed. “You are fortunate to have Gary to share in the raising of your children, and at the risk of sounding insensitive, are there plans for any more? Or are you going to stick with just the two?”

Her eyes clouded for a moment, Candy shrugged. “It’s hard to say. I mean, it really could go either way. I’m thinking about taking next semester off to spend time with Joy, but eventually I’ll finish school, and there’s all the time that each of them will need. Adding another member would only take some of my attention from them, so it’s something we’ll have to consider more deeply before we decide.”

Her features drawn, Lanelle held her tongue. She was not aware her daughter had any such plans for the spring semester, but it wasn’t her place to second guess her choice. Especially not in the company of Gary’s cousins. “I’m sure you’ll make the best choices,” she said almost to herself, aware that Candy rarely decided anything without due deliberation. Her heart swelling with pride, she laid her head back and closed her eyes to listen while the rest enjoyed the afternoon of baby talk and getting to know each other better.

Half an hour later, Annette had taken a turn with the cuddling, then passed the infant to Gary for a change before her feeding. “She’s remarkable,” she praised as she and Bella pulled on their coats. “Please, enjoy your baby girl and don’t let what anyone says interfere with your happiness.”

Moved by her words, Candy stepped forward, accepting the taller woman’s hug. Then, turning to Bella, who already matched her short stature at the age of twelve, she offered, “Come and visit any time.”

“Thank you,” Bella agreed, giving her a firm squeeze as well. The girl had missed New York, but moments such as these eased her suffering. Opening her phone, she admired the pic of her new cousin that she had snapped earlier, then followed her mother out to their car, leaving the youngest Ford to a quiet evening in her new home.

NINE

The Little Things

"WHO THE HELL CAN THAT BE?" Gary grumbled aloud while standing in his kitchen at six in the morning. The doorbell had been a surprise for certain, and he ran his hands roughly through his hair as he considered whether to answer it before he decided that he probably should.

Closing his robe around him, he shuffled through the living area, then peeked out to find Glenda Tucker waiting on the other side of the thick, wooden panel. Securing the tie to hold his cover in place, he twisted the lock and allowed her inside, adding gruffly, "Do you have any idea what time it is?"

"Of course," she replied tartly, her wrinkled lips pursed. "Unscheduled visits can occur at any time, as you well know."

"Yeah, I know," he muttered, returning to the kitchen and adding the powder to the bottle he had been preparing. "Let's go," he instructed as he took to the stairs.

Seated in the rocking chair, Candy did her best to

comfort her as Joylana squirmed, crying out occasionally as she chewed on her fist. "Lookie, honey. Daddy's here with the good stuff," she sang as she accepted the feeding and placed the nipple within reach. "I told you it loses it's luster," she teased, noting his disheveled and somewhat grumpy appearance.

"We have a visitor," Gary stated gruffly, indicating the older woman who had followed him into the room. Leaving them, he used the bathroom to access his own chamber, closing the door behind him with a sharp click.

Noting Glenda for the first time, Candy's eyes grew wide, and she curled her arms tighter around her bundle instinctively, as if to prevent the older woman from snatching her away. "This is a terrible time for an inspection," she gasped, swallowing her fear that it could be more than just a visit.

"It's the perfect time," Ms. Tucker clipped. Shifting her gaze around the dimly lit room, she noted the changes that had been made since her last visit three days prior. A few decorations had been added to the walls, and the curtains on the window were new. "I'll need to give Joy a look, please."

"Certainly," Candy replied stiffly. "After she's eaten, you can have all the looks you want." Her gaze narrowed, she couldn't believe interrupting the meal had even been suggested. She had never been overly fond of Glenda Tucker, and her feelings had been on the downhill slide with every inspection that was made.

"Fair enough," the agent agreed. Continuing her perusal of the nursery, she observed, "I notice you've finished the room a bit more fully. New purchases?"

"Yes. We went shopping to fill in the missing pieces

and give Joy's room a more personal feel. We also had some necessities that were added to get us through the next month or so."

"And she stayed with Carol while you were out?"

"We took her with us," Candice admitted more quietly, her thoughts drawn to their first foray with their new daughter.

Her brow raised, Glenda pivoted to face her. "And how did that go?"

"It went fine," Candy countered, her body stiffened.

"No incidents? Just an ordinary shopping spree."

"Well, I wouldn't call it ordinary," Candy sighed, realizing the other woman may have been spying on them. "We garnered a bit of attention, as I'm sure you can imagine."

Removing her coat, Glenda laid it over her arm and folded it into her lap as she took a seat on the small bench beneath the window. "The first time out is always the hardest. Was it what you expected it would be?"

"Not at all," Candy confessed, her bottom lip quivering. "People stared. A few pointed. Even a few comments were made that we overheard. I didn't realize how rude people could be."

"And now you know," Glenda finished for her.

"Yeah, now we know," Gary tacked on, rejoining them with two cups of coffee in hand. Offering them to each of the women, he sighed loudly. "Any tips for dealing with the nosy, ill-mannered sorts?"

Accepting the warm beverage, Glenda glared up at him. "You seem to be unshaken by the incident."

"Bah." Gerald grinned. "We won't let a little whispering get the better of us."

Sipping noisily from her cup, Candy's eyes met the

wide brown orbs of her daughter. "No, we have no intention of giving up," she stated with more confidence than she felt. Fear still roiled within her that something would happen and Joy would be removed from their home, but she hoped to avoid admitting as much if she could help it.

"Good," Glenda agreed with her first genuine smile since her arrival. "I must admit, the room is looking quite finished. I love the choice of colors." Standing, she opened a few of the drawers in the tall chest, which had previously held only a few items. Moving to the closet, she observed aloud, "Blankets, onesies, even a few dresses. Looks like you are enjoying your daughter, but I should remind you there is more to parenting than playing dress up." She punctuated the directive by closing the narrow door firmly.

"I know how to be a parent," Candy sighed. The bottle almost empty, she held out her mug for Gary to take. "Thanks." Standing, she placed Joylana on the changing table and set the empty bottle aside. "Come and make your inspection," she suggested as she reached for a clean diaper and the wipes. "That way I only have to unwrap her once."

Seizing the opportunity, Glenda hovered over the shorter woman while she changed the diaper. Candy handled the task expertly, her hands confident as they cleaned the small bottom and replaced the diaper. Changing out the clothing, she turned the baby over so her bare back would also be visible before she recovered her in one of the new outfits she had selected during their day out.

"Satisfied?" Gary asked, having remained in the room to quietly observe the exchange.

"She appears to be doing well," Glenda agreed with a loud sigh. Casting her eyes again around the nursery, she emitted the faintest of grins. "I imagine Joylana will be quite happy growing up here."

Her heart pounding, Candy's hands shook as she applied a thin blanket, wrapping her daughter firmly. Swallowing, she held her voice steady as she seconded the notion. "Yes. She is in good hands, and we will do all that we can to give her a happy life."

Not bothering to continue the banter, their social worker exited the room, her eyes darting into the shared bathroom on her way by. Out in the hall, she returned to the stairs and the ground floor, where she made her way to the kitchen and then the laundry room in the basement below with her cup of coffee still in hand.

The couple let her go, helping themselves to fresh cups of coffee and taking seats at their long table. On the other side of the wall, Lanelle would still be sleeping, or at least Candy hoped that she would. Having her rest interrupted always held the potential of interfering with her health, and no one in the household would disturb her if they could help it.

Finishing her warm beverage as she inspected the finished basement, Glenda smiled to herself, relaxing when she realized she had not been followed. She had done her best to appear firm, as letting down her guard would be out of the question. She must remain diligent, observing with a keen eye, never allowing herself to become complacent or overly trusting. It was the hardest part of her job but also the most important, as getting chummy with adoptive parents could put children at risk.

Taking her empty cup to the top of the stairs, she

ensured her scowl had been firmly rooted in place before she closed the door behind her. "I'll be back again between now and Christmas day," she informed the couple as she placed her cup on the table and shoved her arms into her coat. "You have any plans for the holiday?"

"We're going to put up the tree today," Candy informed her. "We've decided to get a real one this year."

"Be sure you watch Joy in case she has any type of reaction."

Chewing her lip, Candy hesitated. "We'll call you right away if anything doesn't seem right."

"And take her to the ER. You can never be too careful," Glenda instructed, not waiting for confirmation that her instructions would be followed before she let herself out the front door.

Staring after her, Gary exhaled loudly, waiting a full minute before he spoke. "I guess she's gone."

"Thank God," Candy mumbled, having gotten a small belch and ready to cradle Joy in a more comfortable position. "Should we risk going back to bed, or are we up for the day?"

"I doubt I could sleep." Gary shrugged. "That woman has always been odd, but now that the baby is here, I think she's only getting worse."

"My, you are all up early," Caroline observed quietly as she joined them.

"Glenda was here," Candy informed her with a sneer. "Another surprise inspection."

"Oh." Carol giggled. "Well, I guess that's her job. It must be hard carrying around so much responsibility."

"I guess that's true," Gary whispered, grinning at

their sleeping babe. "At least Joy doesn't seem to be disturbed by her visits even if the rest of us are."

"I'm not disturbed," Candy disputed. "I just wish they were over already."

"Still afraid something will go wrong and she'll take her away during one of them?" Gary asked.

Pausing, Carol listened to the conversation without comment, as she had not been informed of Candy's fears directly. However, she had sensed the tension in her friend since Joy's arrival and welcomed the insight. Pulling out eggs and bacon, she set about preparing a meal for them.

Her voice quiet, Candy could tell their housemaid was listening. She had not intended to voice her misgivings openly, but it would appear her attempts to keep them to herself were in vain. "I think my fears are justified. After my history with Christmas, it would be about right to lose her, especially on the next visit."

"Oh, Candy," Carol sighed. Placing her skillet on the stove, she glanced at Gary for approval before she added, "Don't worry about the little things. Enjoy your daughter. The holidays aren't after you, despite your previous experiences."

"Easy for you to say," Candy grumbled, using a stiff digit to caress her daughter's cheek. "I'll do my best, but don't be surprised if things take a turn for the worse when you least expect it."

Sharing another glance, neither Carol nor Gary said any more. They shared a secret pact between them, each hoping to help Candy get over her fear of Christmas and life in general. Each of them understood that pushing the matter would only make things worse.

TEN

Not a Date Night

"WHAT AN AMAZING TREE!" Benjamin Monroe observed as he entered via the kitchen. He had parked his car behind the house only a few minutes before and came through the back door as if he were a member of the household rather than a guest.

"Hi, Ben," Candy greeted, her small frame stretched as she added ornaments to some of the taller branches. "Are you and Carol enjoying another non-date night?"

His face slightly flushed, the family attorney grinned. "You know Caroline and I are just friends."

"Yeah, we know," Gary agreed, also adding ornaments to the tree.

"He's going with us tonight," Caroline informed them with a hint of sass. "If that's all right, of course."

"The more the merrier," Gary chuckled, stealing a glance at the other couple. He and Candy gave them a hard time, but their relationship appeared to be strictly platonic, despite the occasional dinner date. "How are things down here?" he asked in a booming voice as he squatted next to Daks, who had been in charge of decorating the lower branches of the tree.

"Pretties," Dakota stated happily. His pudgy fingers had gained a great deal of dexterity over the few years that Gary had known him, and he had successfully added a few dozen balls and shapes to the prickly limbs, albeit the tight clump would probably need a bit of adjustment later.

"Yes, pretties," Candy agreed, grinning from ear to ear as she watched them. Glancing at her daughter, who slept contently in her basinet, a feeling of peace trickled over her. Glenda's visit that morning had put her on edge, but the feeling had slowly subsided as they spent the day at the tree lot making their selection.

Returning home, they had enjoyed a meal followed by hot chocolate and hours of decorating. Her mood had improved immensely, either because of the festive occasion or for the fact that their social worker would not return for several days. Either way, she felt more relaxed than she had since Joy's arrival and couldn't wait for their evening to get under way.

"Have you mapped our route?" Ben asked, followed by a noisy slurp from his hot-toddy.

"Indeed, I have." Gary nodded. Still helping Daks with the finishing touches, he whispered loudly, "Are you ready to go see the Christmas lights?"

"See the 'ights!" Dakota giggled. Leaving his father to the tree, he went in search of his coat, calling, "Mimi, come!"

"I guess that means we're ready to go." Candy laughed. "Are you sure you want to stay behind with the baby?" she asked, turning to her mother with concern in her voice.

Helping her grandson don his outerwear, Lanelle agreed, "Yes. It would be better for both of us if we stayed inside where it's warm. Besides, she just had her bottle half an hour ago and will probably sleep the whole time you're gone."

"Relax," Gary commanded, offering his wife her coat. "She has our number if anything happens, and we'll be gone less than two hours at most."

Candy hesitated, not wanting to spoil the mood of the moment but aware that anything could happen that would delay their return. Holding her smile, she agreed quietly, "Yes, I know. We'll be back before you know it." Resting her hand on her daughter's chest for a moment, she exhaled a calming breath, then shoved her hands into her coat sleeves and followed the others out the back door.

In the garage, Gary started the Suburban and warmed the engine. Backing it out into the drive, he put it in park and climbed out, ready to help get everyone loaded on board.

Taking the farthest back seat, Carol and Ben lay a blanket across their legs. Tugging at the soft material, the young woman pulled it to her chest, hiding her trembling hands underneath. She and Ben had been out several times over the last year, and as far as anyone else was concerned, they were just friends. If she were diligent, she could keep it that way.

In the middle seat, Candy helped Dakota strap into his booster, and Gary added a layer of cover to their laps as well. Tucking the edges around the squirming eight-year-old, he laughed, "Relax, buddy. The lights aren't going anywhere, and you have to stay warm."

"He'll be fine," his wife informed him, then leaned across to give him a quick peck on the cheek.

"Is that my tip?" Gary growled in gravelly tones. His gloved fingers gently brushed the spot her lips had grazed, confident she had no idea the fire she had unleashed with the simple gesture.

"Maybe," Candy teased with a laugh, turning her attention to her own blanket and tacking it into place.

Groaning to himself, Gary returned to his position behind the wheel and called, "All set?" Watching in the rear-view mirror, he could see that everyone appeared comfortable and ready to depart.

"All set," Ben hollered back, twisting and laying his arm across the back of his seat behind Carol.

Hiding her grin, Candy pretended not to notice, focusing her attention on Daks and his excited squeals as the lights floated past. Outside, the air hardly moved, and large flakes of snow floated to the ground. They had seen flurries all day, but as of yet, the ground and streets remained clear.

Closing her eyes, Candy thought about leaving Joy behind with her mother. *Next year, she'll barely be old enough to notice the lights, but the year after that...* Shaking herself back to reality, she put the daydream on hold. It wasn't like her to speculate about the future, as she dreaded the disappointment seeing those dreams dashed could bring.

"Oh, mommy," Daks cooed, squirming against his restraints to see better.

They had turned into a highly affluent neighborhood, and every house on the block had been treated with glowing orbs and plastic lawn ornaments. "Oh, baby," she gurgled back. "Aren't the lights incredible?"

Laughing loudly, Dakota pointed, then chewed eagerly on the finger. Wiping at his drool, Candy grinned at his happiness, knowing the extra saliva was a sure sign of his excitement. Focused on him, she caught the movement in the seat behind them from the corner of her eye, the hand resting on Carol's shoulder and toying with her soft locks most likely thought to be hidden.

Just breathe, Caroline soothed to herself. Next to her, Ben's body pressed against hers beneath the blanket. Across her neck and shoulders, she could feel the weight of his arm and the tingle his fingers sent cascading down her nerves as he toyed with her hair.

Snuggling deeper into the crux of his arm, she flicked her gaze between the window and the display beyond and the back of her boss's head. Sure, she and Candy had become good friends, but the bottom line remained; the Fords were still her employers.

Fingers pried at her elbow, and she reached for them beneath the protection of the blanket, using her right digits to entwine her grasp with Benjamin's left. Stealing a glance at him, she could see his stare hard fixed on the window on that side, but his attention was firmly on her.

She had no idea when this feeling between them had begun to grow. She had worked in his office for four years, and they had held a strictly professional relationship the entire time. Then, after being nearly killed last Christmas by Harvey Waters and his cronies, the couple had ventured into a tentative friendship, but that had folded with the coming winter.

Giving his fingers a squeeze, Carol fought the tears. She had told herself numerous times that he was too old for her, at ten years her senior, but tonight she didn't care. She liked lying against him, enjoying the frost on the windows and the lights in other people's yards.

A loud peal of laughter rang out in the seat in front of her, drawing her back for a moment, out of her daze. Smiling at the little boy whom she cared for day in and day out, she blinked rapidly, a few drops spilling over and wetting her cheeks. No, she couldn't get too lost in this man. Candy and her family still needed her.

Besides, she had been happier in her current position than any other she had ever held. Even working as Ben's secretary couldn't compete. A smile curling her lips, she nestled beneath their blanket and sighed. *Ben isn't going anywhere,* she mused, not willing to consider any possibility to the contrary.

ELEVEN

WooWoos for Sis

"WOW, this Christmas is literally flying by," Gary observed as they enjoyed their breakfast the following morning.

"It sure is," Candy agreed, her attention divided between her meal and the baby resting in her arms.

"You're taking Daks to see Santa this morning, aren't you?" Carol asked as she began the cleanup from the meal.

"Gary is," Candy informed her. "I'm going to stay here and play with the baby," she cooed.

"You hear that, little man? We get a boy's day out!" Gary tussled Dakota's dark locks as he teased him. "Let's grab our coats and get moving before they change their minds."

Giggling at his father's playfulness, Daks squirmed his way out of his chair and took off for the coat closet. Yanking the door open, he reached for his jacket and eagerly accepted it when Gary pulled it down and helped him put it on.

"You won't miss being there for Santa?" Lanelle

asked doubtfully from her favorite seat next to her bedroom door.

"I'm going to make a video," Gary confessed. "I'm sure all of you would like to share in the experience. But dragging everyone out in the fresh snow isn't really practical."

"I know that's right," Carol giggled, recalling the couple of hours they had spent touring the neighborhood the night before. It had snowed on them the entire time, and a light covering had begun to form by the time they returned, which had only grown deeper while they slept.

"Be careful," Candy bade as Gary kissed her on his way out.

"Yes, ma'am." Taking Daks's hand, he led the boy and closed the door firmly behind them.

As soon as they had gone, Lanelle stood and ambled into her bedroom, calling over her shoulder, "I'm going to enjoy a hot soak."

"Ok, mom," Candy sighed, using a finger to play with Joy's lips and chin. She enjoyed the smile her efforts produced. "You sure are a happy baby," she observed quietly.

"I guess that's why her name is so perfect," Carol agreed with a short laugh.

Cutting her eyes over at their housekeeper, Candy's heart raced. "Yes. Joy does suit her well." Hesitating, the moment could not have been more perfect, as she had realized last night that the two of them had needed a few minutes alone to talk. However, she had not expected the time to arrive so quickly or easily. Inhaling deeply, she steeled her nerves. "Carol, would you mind leaving that for a few minutes. If you could sit, I think that we need to have a talk."

Her soapy hands frozen over the sink, Caroline's heart beat loudly inside her chest. "Is something wrong?"

"No, I don't suppose. I just think we need to have a little private girl chat, if you know what I mean," Candy replied, forcing a hint of mystery into her tone.

Drying her palms on a cloth, Carol adjusted her bangs, then took the chair across from her. Slowing her breaths, she considered there were a hundred things her friend might want to discuss, and most of them were no reason to be upset. "Ok, what's up?" she sang.

"I need to speak with you about Ben," Candy stated quietly, her eyes watching through the door and to the bathroom in her mother's suite beyond.

"Ben," Carol gasped, her anxiety renewed. "What about him?"

Candy picked up on the other woman's trepidation, her worst fears confirmed. "Carol, you know we wouldn't try to tell you how to run your life –"

"No, of course not!" Carol interrupted. Wringing her hands, she gushed, "I guess our feelings for each other have been noticed."

"Yeah, they have," Candy agreed, directing her gaze to her best friend. "I'm happy for you. Don't get me wrong. But I'm scared at the same time. When you leave…" Her voice trailed away as a knot formed in her throat and prevented her from putting those fears into words.

"Now wait a minute!" Carol countered, holding up both hands in a stopping motion. "You think that Ben and I are getting serious?"

"Well," Candy hemmed and hawed. "It looked

pretty serious to me. You were rather cozy last night, despite my best efforts not to watch."

Her face flushed, Carol sighed. "Oh, Candy. I'm so sorry. I'm so embarrassed."

"Don't be," her friend laughed. "It's natural to fall in love." Glancing at the babe sleeping on her lap, she whispered, "I just wish the timing could have been better. I really need you right now."

"And you've got me," Carol assured, leaning forward and giving Candy's arm a squeeze. "Ben and I may be on the way to actually dating, but for now, nothing has been declared. We still haven't even kissed if you can believe that!"

"Oh. From the looks of it, I thought…"

"No. Nothing more than a little hand holding," Caroline acknowledged with a small grin. "But I have to admit I've been thinking lately that it just might turn out to be something more."

Picking up on the other girl's distress for the first time, Candy scowled. "Then what's stopping you?" Could Carol be keeping things on hold for her family's sake? *That would be terrible news!*

"Actually, I'm a little concerned about his age," Carol confessed. Standing, she returned to her dishes. "You know he just turned forty-one a few weeks ago."

"Oh," Candy groaned, her reasoning clear. "You think he's too old."

"He is too old," Carol sniffed. "I see you and Gary, growing your family. I never realized how badly I wanted one for myself, but I have to admit I've become a little jealous."

"Oh, Caroline," Candy sighed. Putting Joy on her shoulder, she fought her way to her feet. "Ben is only a few years older than Gary, so I don't think that he's too old. Not in the least. Have you talked with him about it?" she asked, using her free hand to pull her around to face her.

"No," Carol admitted quietly, using the back of her hand to dry her cheeks. "What if he isn't even in the same place? It would spoil everything if I bring it up and he's not ready to discuss it."

Grinning, a warm feeling exploded within Candy's gut. "No one's ever asked me romance advice before."

Coughing a laugh, Carol countered, "Well, I didn't really intend to, but now that I have, what do you think? Is it worth the risk, or should I put a stop to this where it stands? Before it gets out of hand."

Pursing her lips, Candy considered the question. She had her own stakes in the game, so to speak, as having Carol and Ben find love in each other's arms would mean the end of life in the Ford house as they knew it. "It's hard for me to say," she replied gently. "We would hate to lose you."

"Then if you advised against it, it would be for selfish reasons."

"Maybe. But Ben's a good man. And the two of you seem to enjoy each other's company. If I were honest and the kind of friend you deserve, I would have to say you should take it slowly, but he's definitely worth at least the chance." Candy smiled as soon as she had laid out her advice. "Wow, I guess I just gave you my blessing."

"Oh, Candy," Carol squealed, giving her friend a half squeeze with Joylana sandwiched in between. "You are my best of friends, for certain, and I will give it some thought. Maybe in the new year, Ben and I will have time to talk about what each of us wants out of the future and decide if it's worth taking the chance."

Candy leaned into the half hug. "You are welcome, and I hope that it works out even if we lose you in the end. As much as we have loved having you here, we would never want to stand in the way of your future."

"Aww," Lanelle groaned, then giggled at the video being displayed on Gary's phone. They were seated side by side at the kitchen table, with the screen creating dancing light before them.

"Oh, that's nothing. Wait till you see what he did next," Gary informed her with a laugh. Skipping to the next short clip, he tilted the device slightly so that everyone could see as Carol and Candy both anxiously watched from over their shoulders. "Can you see, kitten?"

"Yes, it's fine," Candy whispered, resting her hand on his shoulder. "Thank you for taking him. He seems to have had a great time."

"Oh, he loved it," Gary agreed.

The video changed as the scene zoomed in, with Dakota sitting on Santa's lap. "Need woowoos," Daks said, his hand splayed in the air as he tried to explain his desires to the jolly old elf.

"Woowoos," Santa repeated.

"He wants a new firetruck," Gary's voice intervened from off camera.

"You need a new fire truck!" The old man exaggerated his words, his eyes wide as he played along.

"Woowoos for sis!" Dakota tried again.

"For sis," Gary's words filled the mic again. "Daks, Joy will get her own presents. It's your turn to talk to Santa. Tell him what you want this year."

"Want woowoos!" Daks screamed, anger seeping into his shrill voice. "Joy's woowoos!"

"Fine, fine," the man holding him soothed. "Your sister gets a firetruck. Is there anything else you would like to have?"

Clapping his hands, Dakota appeared content with the promised delivery. "Play Joy'ana," he beamed.

"Oh, God," Candy gasped, tears in her eyes as the image ended. Standing up straight, she covered her mouth with her trembling hand and made a beeline for the office.

Standing in the private space, she allowed the tears to flow freely. Selecting a few tissues, she dabbed at them, then sniffed loudly.

"Are you ok, kitten?" Gary called gently from the door. Even with her back to him, he could tell she was crying.

"He didn't ask for anything for himself," she sniffed.

"Well, not exactly."

"No, exactly. He asked for a gift for Joy," she wailed.

"Yes. And to get to play with her. Isn't that amazing?"

Her lip quivering, Candy hugged herself tightly. "If they take her away, he won't ever get the chance," she observed in a voice almost too low to be heard.

"They aren't going to take her away," Gary soothed, his hands kneading her shoulders.

"You don't know that," she sighed. "Anything could happen."

"Or nothing could happen," he stated firmly, his arms wrapping her tightly and pressing on her chest above her breasts. "Kitten, you have to let it go. Stop being afraid of the what ifs."

"I don't know that I can. I never realized how important this would be to him. I didn't think he would really understand what having a little sister would mean, but he does. He knows who and what she is. It would devastate him to lose her!" Her voice ended in a high-pitched wail.

"He isn't going to lose her," Gary insisted, loosening his grip and forcing her to face him before he enveloped her once more. "She is going to be ours, Candy. Ours for the rest of our lives."

Raising her hands to his back, Candy clung to him, her tears wetting his shirt as she pressed her face into the cotton cloth. "I hope you're right, baby. I know she's only been here a few days, but I think it would break us all if she were to be taken away or if I made a mess of things."

TWELVE

A Mother's Heart

STANDING in the doorway of the kitchen on Christmas Eve, Lanelle leaned against the frame. Wrapping her robe around her, she exhaled a loud sigh.

Before her, Candy sat on the new sofa, cradling Joylana and humming to her softly. Glenda had made her visit a short time ago, and they would probably not see her again until close to New Year's; a fact that did little to ease Candy's tense disposition.

Over her shoulder, the older woman could hear her grandson laughing loudly in the back yard. Gary had taken him out to build a snowman in the thick snow that had coated the ground over the last few days. Smiling to herself, she counted her blessings, as their home was cozy, their belly's full, and their life so much easier than it had once been.

Returning her attention to her daughter and granddaughter, her smile faded. Candy had always struggled with Christmas. Even before Jason was killed, she had taken it hard. Her friends' gifts had always been better. Their adventures and happiness better. Their lives somehow more important. Lanelle hated to admit it, but Candy had always been a glass-half-empty sort of person.

"Is something wrong, mom?" Candy called across the room, having noticed her mother's distant stare.

"No," Lanelle chuckled. "I'm just watching. You seem right at home caring for her."

"It's not like it's hard," Candy countered, lifting Joy to her shoulder and rubbing her back firmly. "She's actually way easier than Daks was."

"And yet you are still afraid of the other shoe," her mother teased.

"Other shoe?" Doubt filled her voice and her mind.

"It's always hanging over you," Lanelle informed her, shuffling in and taking a seat in her designated chair. "For the most part, I've tried to ignore it, hoping it would one day go away."

"I see," Candy sighed, still caressing the small frame in her arms. Her thoughts drifting away, she recalled her argument with Gary only a few days before. *A perfectionist.* That's what he had called her. "Can I help it if I want things to be better?" she defended aloud, not daring to use the word *perfect*.

"No, sweetheart. There's nothing wrong with wanting things to be better," Lanelle agreed with a small laugh. "But we could spend our whole lives focused on it. Waste so much of our time hoping for something bigger and brighter that we forget to enjoy the light that we have."

Her forehead dented with a frown, Candy grunted, "You think I'm unhappy."

"No, I never said that," her mother sighed, almost sorry she had brought it up. "Maybe it's the weather, with the shorter months. Like an annual depression that you suffer from."

"Pfft."

"Don't pfft me, young lady." Lanelle scowled. "A mother's heart knows when her child is hurting. I've seen it with you too many times, but I never could quite put my finger on it. Not until Gary came into your life. Now, it all seems so clear."

"What's so clear, mom," Candy taunted, scooting over and laying Joy on a blanket-covered cushion to change her.

"I think you are afraid of being happy."

A sharp pain stabbed Candy in the chest. Not letting on, she continued with the diaper.

"I mean it, love. You have this dark cloud that follows you around."

"Oh, so now it's my fault that bad things always seem to happen to me."

"Bad things happen to everyone," her mother soothed. "Your father died, it's true, but he was my husband. It happened to me as well."

Stealing glances, Candy didn't dare look at her mother directly. "And?"

"And I know you're afraid of what's going to happen with Joylana," Lanelle finished flatly.

"I'm not afraid," Candy spat, glaring at the older woman. "Why would you even say that?"

"I can see it on you," Lanelle informed her, emitting a small sigh. "Like I said, I hoped that someday you would outgrow it or learn to let it go. But that hasn't happened yet. It scares me to think that this is who you might always be. Always sad when there is so much around you to be happy for."

In an instant, Candy's mind leapt to her grades; her most recent and recurring disappointment. She had worked so hard for them. "I have good reasons to be sad, mom."

"Ok, what are they?"

"Well, the semester is over," Candy hinted.

"And you should be happy that you have finished another one!" her mother rebuked. "With each one that passes, you are closer to earning your degree. I'm so proud of you, baby!"

"Pfft," Candy spit again. "You shouldn't be proud. My grades are hardly anything to write home about," she whined.

"See? That's exactly what I'm talking about," her mother pushed. Raising a hand, she wafted it at her. "You won't accept the success of your… success. You always want it to be something more. The grass is greener syndrome. Remember the year your father built that doll house for you?"

Startled, Candy's eyes grew wide. No. She hadn't thought of it in years. "What about it?" she growled.

"You loved it for all of a day. Then you saw the toys that Katy down the street got, and suddenly it just wasn't good enough."

"I was eight years old, mom. I didn't know any better," Candy replied angrily.

"And you are twenty-three now, and you still don't."

Hearing the pain in her mother's voice, Candy's movements slowed. Wrapping Joy with calculated motion, her thoughts turned. Retracing the last few days, she sighed. "What is it you want from me?"

"I want you to enjoy your life a little, baby. It's way too short to spend it afraid of what might happen. Or worse, always downplaying our treasures because there's a better one out there." Raising her hand, she waved it at the window, indicating the wide world beyond.

Biting her lip, Candy didn't move. What could she say that would explain away her mother's doubts? Finally, she replied softly, "I enjoy my life, mom. But what am I going to do if they suddenly decide to take Joy back?"

"If you live in fear, then they won't have to steal your Joy. You will have given it away all on your own," her mother informed her calmly, turning the pun. "She's your daughter as long as she lives within these walls. We all love her and want her to be a part of our family."

"Exactly."

"Then open your heart and let her in, as well as let the happiness out. Even if something were to happen, the time you shared with her could never be taken away. Make it the best time that you can, and don't worry about it being the ultimate best. Sometimes, most times, just ok is good enough. Enjoy your doll house because it is yours."

Candy coughed a short laugh, thinking of the toy her mother spoke of. It had been a simple thing, and it was true, the one Katy got was twice as big and came with extra furniture and three new dolls to boot. "I never did play with it much," she mumbled.

"And you outgrew it."

"Yeah," Candy sighed, blinking back tears. Folding her arms around Joylana, she stared into her daughter's dark eyes. "She's mine, isn't she." She had been more than willing to give Joy her physical needs, but would she be able to give her the love that would mean just as much?

"Of course she is," Lanelle agreed. "You know, baby, a mother always wants the best for her child even when she doesn't know how to give it to them. And it's ok. It's the effort and the bond that grows between them that matters, no matter how imperfect it is."

"Do you think that's why her real mother gave her away?"

Lanelle flinched at the question, startled by it. "How do you mean?" she whispered.

"Her mother put her in that box. I can't help it. I keep thinking about that, like at some point she will change her mind. She'll come back and want her again."

"I don't think she can do that."

"I know. But what if she did?"

"You mean like Dakota's father, showing up like he did two years ago," her mother deduced.

"Yeah. Maybe." Candy blinked rapidly, tears threatening to give away the depth of her emotions on the subject. "Her mother abandoned her," she managed in a squeaky voice. "How does she ever come back from that?"

The light came on more brightly than Lanelle ever could have imagined. "Oh, honey. She didn't abandon her. Not really. She sent her to you. To a place and a family that could give her all the things she knew that she couldn't."

"It was a selfish thing to do," Candy clipped.

"Oh, I don't think so," Lanelle countered gently. "It was the most selfless thing she could have done. And she named her Joylana. What hope that name holds. What future lies in store."

Droplets of sorrow spilled over, wetting the blanket in her arms. A tiny fist in her mouth, Joy chewed on it, sucking at her fingers. And then she smiled. A brief grin on her lips, Candy inhaled sharply. “She’s so beautiful, mom. I want to be good enough for her.”

“You are good enough, sweetheart. When a mother loves her child and gives with all her heart, it’s always good enough. Face whatever comes with a positive attitude, and never forget that no one can steal your joy, literally, unless you let them.”

THIRTEEN

Smitten

THE FOLLOWING MORNING, Dakota was up with the sun. Bouncing into his parents' room, he squealed, "Santa, Santa! Joy'ana, Santa!"

Sitting up, Candy giggled at his tiny hands grasping the side of her small crib. Giving it a shake, he was calling her to come down and share his happy morning with him. "I think she's a little young for Santa, sweetheart," she soothed, standing and gently removing his fingers from the crib. "Maybe next year she'll be ready to open presents."

Undaunted, Daks grinned up at her. "Happy Momma."

"Happy Momma," she repeated in a hushed voice. Lifting Joy to her chest, she gently kissed the top of her head.

"What's going on?" Gary asked groggily. He had stayed up late and set everything up downstairs before bed, allowing Candy to retire early. He had obviously not gotten enough sleep.

"Someone's awake and ready for Santa," she beamed.

Throwing the covers back, Gary placed his bare feet on the floor, welcoming the cold, hard wood. "Then let's not disappoint him, shall we?" Pulling on his robe, he offered his hand. "Come on, little man. Let's see what he brought us."

Gathering a clean diaper, wipes, and a blanket, Candy followed with the baby. Giving Carol's door a gentle knock, she announced through the wood covering, "We're up!"

"So I hear." Caroline's laughter tinkled from the other side. "I'm going to grab a shower, and I'll be down to make breakfast in a few minutes."

"Take your time," Candy hollered back, fairly certain it would be a while before anyone was really hungry. Making it to the bottom steps, she paused, her jaw dropping open in disbelief. "What on Earth!" she gasped.

Seated in her living room were Roger and Eveline Ford.

"Surprise," the couple shouted in unison.

"Su-pise," Dakota echoed, throwing his hands up and jumping a few times.

"When the hell did you get here?" Candy gasped, clearing the last few steps and shuffling towards them.

"Just after midnight," Eve confessed, reaching for her new granddaughter. "Mohammad and the mountain…"

"I've heard it," Candy sighed, passing the infant over.

"Oh, she's beautiful," Eve observed airily.

Cutting her eyes over at her husband, Candy

grinned. "No wonder it took you so long to set up last night."

"Guilty," Gary laughed, indicating her end of the sofa. "Have a seat, kitten. Santa was extra busy this year."

Taking her seat, Candy giggled at his silliness, observing as her mother-in-law perched on the edge of the ottoman. Across from her, Roger was equally smitten, using his fingers to tickle Joy's chubby cheeks and elicit covert smiles.

"What's going on?" Lanelle asked as she joined them, not appearing surprised at their visitors.

"Christmas, what else?" Eve teased, her tone lighter than Candy had previously thought possible.

"We're glad you made it," the girl soothed, accepting packages from her mate. "You brought all this with you?" she asked more quietly so Dakota wouldn't hear.

"Much of it, yes," Roger confessed. "Having grandchildren is such a joy, no pun intended."

Eve laughed, nodding as she added, "It really put me in the giving spirit this year."

"So much you couldn't stay away," Candy surmised as Eveline handed Joylana back to her.

Her hands freed, Eve sat on the floor next to Dakota and joined in his unwrapping. Ripping at the colored paper, he grunted and strained, then clapped with glee when the packaging had been torn away and a new toy revealed.

Spying the gift he had asked for in honor of Joy, he began to shout, "Woowoos, Joy'ana! Sissy woowoos!"

Craning her neck, Candy could see the pink fire

engine still within the box. "I'll be damned," she muttered. "They do make fire trucks for girls!"

"Sure they do," Gary replied with a wicked laugh. "Our little girl is going to love them just as much as her daddy and big brother do!"

"I hope that she does, too," Candy whispered almost to herself as she rested back into her seat.

From the kitchen, Carol peeked out and called, "Anyone ready for breakfast? Or are we having cereal and wait for the big meal later today?"

"I don't know about breakfast, but I'd sure love some coffee and a bottle of formula," Candy called back, still in awe of the scene before her.

"Coming right up!" Carol agreed to the task.

From her seat next to the fire, Lanelle grinned, glad to see her daughter looking so happy. She had known since yesterday that the Fords would be arriving and had struggled to hold the surprise. Shifting her gaze to Gary, who was still distributing the gifts, she sighed, perfectly content to enjoy the moment and happiness only the love of family could provide.

Reaching the bottom of the stack, Gary took a step back. Accepting a mug of fresh brew from their housekeeper, he took up post next to the coat closet and leaned against the wall to observe. Watching his parents and son opening and examining gifts, he smiled. Then shifting his gaze to his bride, the grin slowly disappeared.

All was right with the world as far as everyone else was concerned, but Gary feared that Candy might be having second thoughts about Joy. Things had been hard on her since the baby's arrival, and he knew that caring for her might be more than she was ready to handle despite her best intentions.

Taking a sip from his warm cup, his mind wandered, and he recalled the day they had decided to adopt. So many hard-fought days and hours of work in preparation had gone into the process; it had never occurred to him that it might not be what Candy really wanted. Giving his head a shake, he dragged himself back to the present and the happy scene before him.

Thinking of their more recent conversations, he understood her fears. He had fears of his own, after all. What if she were right and he had let his desire to help others cloud his judgement?

What if I've put too much pressure on her to stay with our plan? Shouldn't she have a right to change her mind if she doesn't think she can handle it? Sadly, it went against all that he was to force her to try.

Shifting his gaze and thoughts once more, he watched as Joy was passed to Lanelle to enjoy her feeding. The entire family had been drawn in by their ebony angel. Not a one of them cared about her differences, like the color of her skin, or what she might require down the road. She had come to their family to be an equal part of them, but they each must accept her and be ready to provide whatever she needed. Forcing Candy to keep that promise if she had given up could have dire consequences for them all, especially the sweet and innocent little girl that had already lost one foster home because the couple couldn't cope with her.

FOURTEEN

A New Plan

CANDY LOOKED around at the smiling faces. Her living room had never been so crowded, or so full of love, on Christmas morning. The tree they had decorated as a family loomed in the corner, its lights twinkling and reflecting off the layers… Gary's at the top, Dakota's decorations bunched in a small patch at the bottom, and hers sandwiched in between.

Tears filled her eyes as she realized that in a few years, part of the tree would be given to Joylana to decorate. *My Joy,* she breathed to herself. She had been letting fear and doubt chip away at her, but her mother was right. *They can only steal my joy if I let them.* She smiled at the play on words, briefly wondering if it would ever grow old.

"Are you ok?" Gary asked, taking a perch on the arm of the sofa and leaning over her. The glistening in her eyes bothered him, and he wished he could make her understand. To give her confidence that it all would work out as it should, and he would support her no matter what path she chose.

"I'm fine," she replied. Placing her hand in his, she squeezed firmly, her smile a sharp contrast to her tears. "I understand now. At least I think I do."

Stretching, she met his lips for a brief kiss, then scooted to the edge of the sofa to stand. Waving her hands above her head, she clapped a few short pops and said in a booming voice, "If I could have your attention, everyone, I'd like to say a few things."

Silence fell over the group. It wasn't like Candice Parker Ford to demand the center of attention. To the contrary, it was more like her to slip away and hide in a back room, as if afraid to even be seen.

"You have something to share, my child?" Eve prompted, her elegant poise always present, even sitting on the floor and opening gifts with her grandson.

"I do," Candy breathed. "I've had a lot on my mind these last few weeks." She fidgeted with her sweater, picking at the pattern. Lifting her chin, she forced a wide smile. "But I'm clear now, or clearer than I was. I know what it is I want to achieve, and I know I can't get there alone."

Across from her, her mother groaned, "Oh, darling," filling the pause. Clasping her hands together, Lanelle waited, holding her breath in anticipation of her daughter's words.

"Thanks, mom," Candy continued. "You have always been there for me even when things were hard. We've been through a lot together, and I know I never could have made it without you."

"Hear, hear," Roger toasted, raising his mug of coffee to the women who shared his son's life.

"Thanks, dad," Candice beamed. "You are all so special to me, and I think I've made a mistake. I should have trusted you sooner. Should have believed in Gary's family… my family… from the beginning." Inhaling deeply, she dove in. "I've wanted to make you all proud of me. To feel like I had earned my place here among you."

"Oh, Candy," Eveline sighed.

"I know," Candy raised her hands, cutting her off. "Having Joy here has made me realize the truth. I never needed to earn it. You have all been my foundation even when I was trying so hard to make it on my own. That's why I'm going to take some sage advice that has been given to me, both from my mother, and the mother who accepted me even with all my flaws. I never have fully thanked you for what you did for me, or for us, at our wedding. I should have known then, but I wasn't ready. Now I'm ready. In the spring, I'm going to pretty much take the semester off."

A gasp escaped a few of the listeners, filling the room for a moment before it fell again to a tense silence.

"I'm not quitting," she promised. "I'm going to take one class for grammar and editing. This whole time, I have struggled with my writing, and I'm ready to admit that I'm not ready for college-level work, at least not as ready as I want to be. I'm going to take a remediation class offered by the college. It's full of kids straight out of high school who are trying to make up for what they missed. I think I'll fit right in, and I'm going to give it my best to make up for all the things getting a GED doesn't prepare you for. Like college."

Her lips parting into a wide smile, she added, "And of course, that means I'm going to have lots of time for Joylana. I've been afraid that someone will decide I'm not good enough to be her mother, but quite honestly, I dare them to try. I want this. I want to be there for her, and I dare anyone to try and take her from me."

"Oh, Candy," her mother squealed, unable to contain herself any longer. Fighting her way to her feet, Lanelle shuffled over, wrapping her arms around her only child. "I'm so proud of you," she whispered against her ear, her forehead pressing against Candy's.

"I know, mom," Candy sighed. "I know that you all are, and I appreciate all the love and support each and every one of you has shown me. And next fall, I'll be ready to dive back in, hopefully with some better results!"

Her confidence filling the room, the gathering cheered for her, with smiles and toast all around. Standing to tower over them, Gary wrapped both of the women in his massive arms, holding his bride against his broad chest.

"I sure do love you, kitten," he confessed. "I'm glad you've decided not to give up."

"I could never give up," she giggled. "No matter how scary Christmas can be, I know now that I can face it. Especially now that I have found my Christmas Joy."

FIFTEEN

Pillow Talk

"DID YOU HAVE A GOOD CHRISTMAS, KITTEN?" Gary asked as he slipped between their sheets and adjusted the blanket over him.

Sitting on her side, Joy nestled at her breast, Candy smiled down at her daughter's dark eyes. Her lips firmly latched onto the nipple of her bottle, she was enjoying her final feeding before the couple turned in for the night.

"I really did," Candice replied with a sigh. "I hate to say I was surprised, but once I made up my mind about Joylana and our future, everything just seemed to click. This could be the best Christmas I've ever had."

"I'm glad," Gary agreed, stretching out and adjusting the covers over him. "We have another week before I go back to work. Is there anything else we need to do during that time?"

"I don't know," she replied deviously, cutting her eyes over at him. "I think we should plan a little New Year's and anniversary combo. That is if Carol wouldn't mind taking care of the four-a.m. feeding for us one night next week."

"Oh," he breathed, leaning towards her and using the backs of his fingers to trail a path down her arm. "Is momma feeling sexy?"

Grinning, Candy slurred, "Maybe. Or just feeling alive. We avoided a Christmas disaster this year, and we gained a beautiful new family member. I think that's something to celebrate."

Dropping the subject, Gary propped himself up on an elbow and looked at her squarely. "Ok. What gives. Where did this change of heart really come from?"

"My mother," Candy admitted quietly. "Well, mostly my mother. She was telling me about how I'm always afraid of things. Or pessimistic about things."

"Like Christmas."

"Exactly like Christmas," Candy admitted softly, a warm flush staining her cheeks. "Save nearly being killed last year and the fire that destroyed our apartment, things probably weren't near as bad as I have always perceived them to be."

"Mmmhmm. You know, we've had that talk before," he accused. "What made her words of wisdom so special."

"The timing, I guess," she added confidently. The bottle empty, she placed it on the night stand and lifted Joy to her shoulder. "She helped me to understand what you were really getting at by calling me a perfectionist. It's not that I want everything to be perfect. It's just that I judge myself so harshly. Harder than anyone else ever would."

"Tell me something I don't know," he grunted.

"I'm sorry. You did try to tell me, but I really do

understand now. I shouldn't waste my chances to do things with my family, and I'm going to do a better job of making time for you guys instead of hiding behind my work or my school. I need to balance things better, and I'm ready to really make the effort to do that."

"That's funny. I think my parents are learning the same thing. Almost like you all got a good dose of Christmas magic this year."

"Christmas magic," Candy said with a laugh. "Let's not get too carried away. And why would you think that your parents are learning anything?" Candy clipped, having earned a belch and standing to lay their daughter down.

"Mom and Dad showing up back here for Christmas is damned unheard of. I think that it may be time for them to stop flying south for the winter," he teased.

"Snowbirds. I remember." Gary had explained the term to her three years ago when they first came to stay with him. "So I guess there are lots of things changing around here."

"A few things," Gary muttered, enjoying the view of her rear as she bent over the basinet to tend to their daughter. "Do you have any idea what you do to me, Mrs. Ford?"

Catching the air in his voice, she peeked at him from the side, but not turning around. "Are you flirting with me?"

"Always," he breathed, tossing back the covers and curling his fingers to entice her to join him.

Seeing that Joy had drifted off to sleep, Candy giggled, "We have about four hours. Are you sure you want to spend that time making love? Sleep is a real commodity these days."

On his knees in an instant, Gary caught her hand and pulled her into the bed. “I’m always up for making love to my wife,” he whispered, then planted a kiss on her that curled her toes and made her forget all about the sleep she would be missing.

Epilogue

TAKING a long drag from her cigarette, Glenda Tucker watched the trees on the far side of the parking lot sway in the morning breeze. Flicking the ash, she grinned, drawing the fine lines around her mouth taut. "Candy and Gary," she muttered as she dropped the butt in the receptacle and made her way inside the building that held the adoption agency facilities.

"What time is Joylana's case on the docket for?" she asked calmly as she passed the receptionist at the front desk.

"Two-thirty," the young woman replied. "Judge Hammond's clerk has already confirmed."

"Good," Glenda agreed with a deep sigh. They had reached the end of a very long journey, or at least her part of it. For six months, she had been making appearances at the Ford residence to check on the infant and watch as things unfolded, and it was time for her to make her recommendations to the court.

Strutting down the narrow hall to her office in the back, she shoved her lighter into her pocket and took a seat at her desk. Pulling the keyboard closer, she wriggled her fingers to warm them and prepared to type.

"Let's see here," she whispered to herself. Searching the directory, she located the proper form and loaded it onto the screen. Filling in the details, she prepared the endorsement she would be presenting in a few hours. "Adoptive parents, Gerald Ford and Candice Parker Ford. Adoptee, Joylana Faith Doe."

Pausing, she stared at the next section. Her notes from each of her visits lay in a folder, which she opened to refresh her memory. "Visits one through three were tense. A short adjustment period compared to some," she observed.

Recalling the one after New Year's, she grinned as she skimmed the page. "After that, it was smooth sailing."

Returning to the keyboard, she typed furiously:

Joylana has been given as near a perfect match as I can imagine. The house has remained safe, and the family is seamless, or as close to it as I can tell.

The older boy, Dakota, is highly protective of the infant and appears to harbor no ill effects from her arrival. His disabilities have had no interference in the transition, and he will be a supportive influence in his role as sibling to the adoptee.

Candice cut back on her school hours and has devoted a large portion of her time to the family life. The early trepidation that I noted on her part was put aside early on, and she has flourished in the care of Joy and her growing family.

Gerald has continued his position with the fire department, where he is still the chief at the firehouse on Pecan street. No ill effects from his employment have been noted, and his family remains a priority in his life as far as I can tell.

The monetary status of the household remains solid, as the family's sizable wealth remains intact and augmented by Gary's income.

From what I have seen, Joylana will enjoy financial stability, loving parents, and a supportive family structure.

It is with my full confidence that I endorse the adoption of Joylana by the Ford family on this 12th day of June, in the year 2019.

Sincerely,

Glenda Tucker

Licensed Master Social Worker for the State of New York

Printing the page, Glenda stared at it, reading her words again before she selected a pen and inserted her signature. Folding the page, she recalled how hard it had been to hold her stern countenance with the Ford family over the weeks and months of her observations.

But that's my job, after all, she mused. To act as an observer only and not influence the choices or actions of those she monitored. *But I'm still glad it worked out.* She had been afraid at first that it wouldn't, with the racial differences that the family would face. *And still will.*

Not to mention the distinct personalities of Gary and Candy. She grinned broadly as she recalled the maturity that had settled over Candice since she had known her. *She's really coming into her own.* Glenda knew that the young woman intended to return to full time student status in the fall, armed with better skills and deeper motivations. *I think she'll make it.*

With a contented sigh, Glenda finished folding the sheet of paper and placed it in an envelope, ready to be delivered. Her final act in the Ford family drama. In the end, she had done what she could for the young family and wished them the best of luck in the years to come.

Thank You

Thank you for reading, and I hope that you have enjoyed the 2018 installment of the Sweet Christmas Series. Look for a new adventure for Gary and Candy at Christmas next year. ~ Sam

Books in this series include:

- Christmas Candy (2015)
- Christmas Eve (2016)
- Christmas Carol (2017)
- Christmas Joy (2018)
- Christmas Holly (2019)
- Christmas Lane (2020)

About the Author

Anyone who knows me could tell you, I am a friendly kind of person, never met a stranger and take up conversations anywhere at any time. I work hard, and my mind never seems to shut down, as I wake up often in the middle of the night with ideas pouring out and demanding to be dealt with. Of course that means much of my books were written in the middle of the night.

I grew up and still live in the great state of Texas where everything is bigger, where we have warm weather and a central location. I love my state, my town, and my family, which includes my four sons, my significant other, and many friends as well.

I have thoroughly enjoyed writing this story and hope that you will love reading it just as much. And of course, there will be many more adventures to come.

You can follow Samantha Jacobey at:
Website: www.SamJacobey.com
Facebook: https://www.facebook.com/SamJacobey
Twitter: https://twitter.com/SamJacobey

Also by SAMANTHA JACOBEY

http://www.amazon.com/-/e/B00GEB5LX0

A New Life Series – an epic adventure, TORI FARRELL's life IS one wild story... escaped from a biker gang and running from drug lords... used by the FBI and hoping to protect her present from her past... IT'S DARK - IT'S BRUTAL, and it's WORTH EVERY MINUTE OF IT!! (Mature read, 18+ for graphic sexual content and violence, including rape)

Summer Spirit Novella Series - no one EVER had a summer romance like this… Charlie visits another plane, parallel to our own, where Summer Angels and Dark Angels battle over the fate of man. A unique twist on an old idea that will keep you guessing; will Charlie and Clarisse ever find their HEA? (New adult)

Teach Me to Prey – in this standalone thriller, JASON TRUITT and his friends have gotten their way for years. Deceit, sex, and foul play aren't normally covered in the curriculum, but they're doing whatever it takes to get under BECKY STEWART's skin. When one of the boys turns up dead, it's a race against time to save the others; a STUNNING STORY that will get your heart racing and leave you breathless by the end… (New Adult)

The Binding (Unexpected Magic #1) - One cursed diary will change two strangers forever...Can Meri and Rider use her mother's old book to figure out why someone is after them? Or will the guilty party succeed, ripping the tome away before killing them and then slithering back into the darkness… (New Adult)

The Wicked Awakened (Unexpected Magic #2) – a Halloween novel; a five-hundred-year-old witch wants to turn SARAH MATTHEWS' body into her new home… A twisted tale involving a coven hell bent on seeing that she succeeds. Who will come out on top in this epic battle of wills? (Mature read, 18+ for graphic sexual content and violence)

The Irrevocable Series - From affluent beginnings, BAILEY DEWITT's life has become a broken mess... after her parents died unexpectedly, she didn't think it could get any worse. But when the arrogance of man catches up and puts the entire world into a dooms-day spiral, there will be only ONE PLACE she can run to - the ONE PLACE she wanted desperately to escape. (New Adult)

The Dragon of Eriden Series - Amicia Spicer led a simple life, until she discovered it had all been a lie… On her deathbed, Arely Spicer confessed to her only daughter that she had been found by, not born to her mother and father. Sad news to be certain, the idea of having a family of flesh and blood waiting to be reunited sent the young, independent woman on the adventure of a lifetime. Little did she know, a dragon's heart beat within her chest and her journey would be more perilous than she could have imagined... (New Adult)

Also from our Lavish family

Love on the Double Duo
By L.A. Remenicky
http://mybook.to/LoveOnTheDoubleDuo

The Monroe brothers fall fast, they fall hard, and they fall forever. But the road to true love isn't always easy.

Loving Jessie's Girl – Book 1: Until AJ Monroe left Indiana after college he had always lived in his identical twin brother's shadow. He had made a life for himself in Denver, Colorado, away from Jessie, away from Indiana. But when AJ feared for his brother's safety, he left everything behind to step back into the shadow he thought he had outgrown. Finding his brother was AJ's only concern...until he met Jessie's girl.

Fiercely independent, Rina Abbot hid her true situation from everyone, including her best friend, Jessie. Out of money and unable to care for her rescue dogs she had no choice but to accept the help of the handsome stranger with a familiar face. Afraid to trust him, she tried to ignore the feelings he stirred within her as they searched for his missing brother.

But secrets never stay secrets for long.

Finally open about their feelings for each other, Rina's secrets began to wreak havoc on their lives. Would Rina's secrets force AJ to give up his dream of loving Jessie's girl?

Beyond Duty – Book 2: After serving in the Marine Corps, Jessie Monroe has finally found a life beyond war. He's focused on

being an EMT and helping his best friend rescue dogs, until he happens upon a curvy blonde stranded

with a flat tire and no jack.

On the run from her past, Dori Graham is slow to trust any man, and she tries to ignore the spark of

interest she feels for her handsome savior, but a friendship grows between them.

When Dori's past invades her new life, Jessie vows to rescue her. Saving her will take him beyond duty

and into his own personal hell. Calling upon his training as a Marine and the depth of his feelings for

Dori, Jessie will need the mental strength to battle to save her and, ultimately, save himself.

Between the Trees
Kathy Moczerniak
http://mybook.to/betweenthetrees

A beautiful coming of age with a dark side that one teenager must fight to overcome…

Beyond Kathryn Lucas' first memory of her father's tree lay a dysfunctional path of violence, heartbreak, and secrets within a family severely entrenched in the vicious cycle of abuse. A lifetime of fear drives her from her home, and the teenage girl finds refuge with an aunt and uncle determined to protect their niece.

Distressing flashbacks unravel in Kathryn's fragile mind among the turmoil encircling her as she struggles through adolescence and descends into her pain-ridden past. When the summation of her unsettling memories allows the darkness to overtake her, she becomes desperate to unearth the light.

Inspired by a true story, Kathryn must hold on tightly to those who love her, searching for her place in a world threatening to break her as she fights to overcome life's betrayals before she is deprived of her future.

The Hunter Series
Sara J. Bernhardt
http://mybook.to/HuntersTril

Jane Callahan is a reclusive, seventeen-year-old high school student dealing with the death of her beloved brother. Her home in Southern California with her mother is a constant reminder of her loss and pain. In hopes of escaping her past she moves to North Bend Oregon to live with her father, where she meets a beautiful boy named Aidan Summers.

Jane is intrigued by his looks as well as his unusual ways of attempting to get her attention. After months of uncommon conversation and frustration, an uncertain romance brews between Jane and Aidan, but Aidan has a ghastly secret that could destroy everything.

www.ingramcontent.com/pod-product-compliance
Lightning Source LLC
Chambersburg PA
CBHW051253170626
46809CB00004B/1626
* 9 7 8 1 9 4 4 9 8 5 6 7 7 *